Notebooks of a Middle-School PRINCESS

Meg Cabot (her last name rhymes with habit, as in 'her books can be habit-forming') is the author of The Princess Diaries series as well as several other series and bestselling novels for children, teenagers and adults. Her books have sold millions of copies around the world. She has lived in various parts of the US and France, but now lives in Key West, Florida, with her husband and her one-eyed cat, Henrietta.

Books by Meg Cabot

The Princess Diaries series

Visit www.megcabot.com to find out
more about Meg's books for all ages

Notebooks of a Middle-School PRiNCESS

Written and illustrated by

MEG CABOT

MACMILLAN CHILDREN'S BOOKS

First published in the US 2015 by Feiwel and Friends

First published in the UK 2015 by Macmillan Children's Books
an imprint of Pan Macmillan
a division of Macmillan Publishers Limited
20 New Wharf Road, London N1 9RR
Associated companies throughout the world
www.panmacmillan.com

ISBN 978-1-4472-8065-1

1 3 5 7 9 8 6 4 2

A CIP catalogue record for this book is available from
the British Library.

Book design by April Ward

Printed and bound by CPI Group (UK) Ltd, Croydon CR0 4YY

'It would be easy to be a princess if
I were dressed in cloth of gold, but it is
a great deal more of a triumph to be one
all the time when no one knows it.'

– Frances Hodgson Burnett
A Little Princess

Wednesday 6 May
9.45 a.m.
Biology Class

Middle school has not been working out the way I hoped it would.

Of course, my expectations were somewhat high. I'd heard such great things. Everyone always goes, 'In middle school you get to do this,' and 'In middle school you get to do that.'

No one ever told me, 'In middle school Annabelle Jenkins is going to threaten to beat you up by the flagpole for absolutely no reason.'

But that's exactly what happened just now when Annabelle Jenkins shoved me in the hallway after second period.

My first thought was that it all had to be a mistake. What have I ever done to Annabelle Jenkins?

That's why I said, 'That's OK!' to Annabelle as I squatted down and gathered up the pages that had spilled from my organizer. I checked and saw that my pink schedule was still taped to the inside cover. Phew!

I know it's weird that it's May and I still worry about losing my class schedule, but I can't help it. You get a demerit if you lose your class schedule. I've gone the whole year without getting a demerit.

Plus I like knowing my schedule is there inside my organizer just in case I suddenly get amnesia or something.

'Don't worry,' I assured Annabelle as I stood up. 'I still have my schedule.'

That's when Annabelle did something really weird. And I mean *really* weird, especially for the most popular, prettiest girl in the sixth grade at Cranbrook Middle School.

She shoved me again!

She did it hard too. Hard enough so that I lost my balance and fell flat on my butt in front of everyone.

It didn't hurt (except for my pride).

But it was still totally shocking, considering that, up until that moment, I'd always thought Annabelle and I were friends. Not *good* friends – we don't sit together at lunch or anything. Annabelle is very selective about who she invites to sit at her table.

But we certainly aren't enemies. We've been to each other's houses, since my step-uncle works with

Annabelle's dad. Whenever I go to Annabelle's, she shows me all the awards she's won for gymnastics, and when

she comes to my house I show her my wildlife drawings. She's never been very impressed by them, but I always thought things were cool between us.

I guess not.

'I'm not worried about you losing your schedule,' Annabelle sneered. 'You think you're so great, don't you, *Princess Olivia*?'

'Whoa,' I said, straightening up. 'Annabelle, are you OK?'

The reason I asked this is because there was no reason that I could think of for Annabelle Jenkins to:

1. Knock my organizer from my arms.

2. Shove me.

3. Ask me if I think I'm so great.

4. Call me a princess.

I thought maybe she'd just found out her dog had been run over or something, and she was taking it out on me. If she even had a dog, which I wasn't sure about. I hadn't seen one the last time I'd been at her house. I like dogs, so I probably would have noticed.

But I guess I was wrong about us getting along, since the next thing that happened was that all of Annabelle's equally pretty, popular friends – who'd gathered around and were watching Annabelle humiliate me – laughed even harder as Annabelle imitated what I'd asked her, using a high-pitched, whiny voice that I personally don't think sounds anything like me.

'Whoa, Annabelle, are you OK?' Annabelle pointed at me, but glanced at all her friends. 'Olivia is such a loser – she thinks I actually like her. She thinks we're friends.'

The look on Annabelle's face made it very clear that we were not now, nor had we ever been friends. We'd probably never even got along.

Then Annabelle leaned her face very close to mine and said, 'Listen here, *Princess Olivia Grace*

Clarisse Mignonette Harrison – *if* that's even your real name, which I doubt. I'm sick of you thinking you're so much better than me. Meet me at the flagpole as soon as school lets out today. I'm going to give you the beat-down you deserve. And if you tell a teacher I'll make sure to say you started it, and *you'll* be the one to get a demerit.'

Then she gave me one more shove – not as hard as the last one – and disappeared, with her friends laughing behind her, into the throng of scarily tall seventh and eighth graders, who take up so much more space in the hallways than us lowly sixth graders.

Fortunately by that time my friend Nishi had come up alongside me.

'What was *that* about?' Nishi asked.

'Annabelle says she's going to give me the beat-down I deserve after school,' I said. I guess I was still in shock, or something. It felt like I was watching myself in a movie. 'She called me a princess.'

'Why would she call you a princess?' Nishi wanted to know. 'And why would she want to give you a beat-down? I thought you two got along.'

'So did I,' I said. 'I guess I was wrong.'

'That's weird. Does she think you're a snob, or something?'

'Why would she think I'm a snob?' I looked down at my clothes, which are the same as Nishi's, since we have to wear uniforms to our school, which include a skirt. I'm not wild about the skirts, which have pleats in them. Pleats are generally not flattering, according to my step-cousin Sara's fashion magazines. 'Do I *look* like a snob?'

'I don't think so,' Nishi said as people streamed around us, trying to get to their next class before the bell rang. 'Not any snobbier than usual.'

I gave Nishi a sarcastic look. 'Gee. Thanks.'

'Well, sometimes people who like sports think people who like to draw wildlife illustrations are—'

'But I've never been snobby about my drawings! It's just a hobby. It's not like I've won any medals for them.'

'Hmm. Weird. Maybe you should tell a teacher.'

'Annabelle said if I did she'd say I started it and make sure I got a demerit. I've gone the whole year without getting a demerit.'

'Why would they believe Annabelle and not you?' Nishi asked.

'Probably because Annabelle's dad's a lawyer,' I reminded her glumly. 'Remember? She's always saying her dad will sue the school if things don't go her way.'

'Oh, right,' Nishi said, shaking her head. 'I forgot. Well, I'm sure it's just a misundertanding. We'll figure it out at lunch. See you then.'

'See you,' I said, not feeling quite as hopeful.

Then we both dived into the hallway throng, since we didn't want to be late. At Cranbrook Middle School, if you're late to class, you lose a merit point. If you lose enough merit points, they won't let you pass on to seventh grade.

Now I'm sitting here still trying to figure out what I could have done to make Annabelle hate me so much, much less want to give me a beat-down.

But I'm coming up with nothing.

Nothing except the fear that after school I'm going to die.

Wednesday 6 May
10.50 a.m.
French Class

The thing is, I'm so completely boring and average. It doesn't seem like there's any reason for Annabelle to hate me.

Me: Olivia Grace Clarisse Mignonette Harrison (my real name, no matter what Annabelle thinks)

Height: Average (for my age, twelve)

Weight: Average (completely within normal body mass index for my height)

Hair: Average colour (brown) and length (to the shoulders, though usually I wear it in braids because it's easier to manage since it has a tendency to frizz, especially on humid days, which, here in New Jersey, happen a lot)

Skin: Average (well, brown, the result of an African-American mom and a Caucasian dad)

Eyes: Average – not sapphire blue, like my step-cousin Sara's, or deep brown, like Nishi's. My eyes are hazel. Just plain, average in-between hazel. They don't even change colour in the light, like girls' eyes do in books, flashing emerald green when I'm angry or anything. They stay hazel all the time.

So. Boring.

There are only two things about me that aren't average, but I don't think they're the reasons why Annabelle wants to beat me up.

The first is my name: Olivia Grace Clarisse Mignonette Harrison (which for some reason Annabelle thinks is fake, but I swear it's not).

I don't know why my mom chose to give me so many middle names, especially such bizarre ones. Mignonette is a sauce you can order in restaurants to put on oysters.

I don't even like oysters.

And there is a famous princess who my step-cousin Sara likes to follow on the gossip blogs named Princess Amelia 'Mia' Mignonette Grimaldi Thermopolis Renaldo, whose grandmother is named Clarisse, so it's like I have two royal middle names (Clarisse and Mignonette), which I will admit is also a bit weird. Sometimes I wonder if my mom was obsessed with princesses or something.

But I can't ask her because she died when I was a baby. I never got a chance to know her, which is too bad, since she sounds like someone I would have liked. She was a charter jet pilot. That's a person who flies private planes for other people.

She didn't die flying, though. She died on vacation in Mexico after crashing her jet ski.

I have never been on a jet *or* a personal watercraft. My aunt says they're more dangerous than flying a private plane.

That is the second non-average thing about me. Since my mom is dead, I have to live with my aunt and her husband and his two kids, my step-cousins Justin and Sara. I've never even met my birth dad, although he sends me letters and stuff. I write back, to a post office box in New York City, because Dad has to travel all the time for his job (for which he gets paid very well. I know, because Aunt Catherine is always super excited when his support check for me comes every month, even though she and Rick, her husband, have a very successful home design and construction business).

This is why I've never met him (my dad, I mean). An assistant forwards him my letters from the post office box. He lives wherever his suitcase happens to be, which is usually somewhere like Costa Rica or

Abu Dhabi (at least according to his postcards).

This is 'an unstable atmosphere in which to bring up a child', according to my aunt Catherine.

My aunt Catherine and my step-uncle, Rick, provide a stable enough atmosphere in which to bring up a child, I guess, but sometimes I wish I could live with my dad. I know we'd have the best times on his archaeological digs, even though there aren't any schools or clean drinking water, only mosquitoes and, according to one movie I saw, mummies.

OK, Dad's never specifically *said* he's an archaeologist, and Aunt Catherine doesn't like it when I ask questions about him, but I'm pretty sure that's how he and my mom met. She had to have been the pilot on one of his expeditions.

That's probably why my dad can only communicate with me by letter. Seeing me in person would be too painful a reminder of all that he lost (not that I'm beautiful like my mom was, because I'm so average-looking, but my aunt Catherine says I have my mother's bone structure and could grow up to be attractive some day).

It's all good, though. Dad explained that when I get lonely or frustrated I should pour out my feelings in my diary (which he sent me – although I never seem to have it with me when I need it, so I just write in whatever is handy, such as my French notebook, like now).

Dad says he knows someone who kept a diary for a long time, and it always helped her. I assume he's referring to my mother, and he just can't bear to say her name (which is Elizabeth) because her beauty haunts him.

Still, even though I never mention this in my letters to my dad, the thing I get *most* frustrated about is that I am basically half an orphan.

Not that anyone ever treats me this way, of course. No one ever forces me to sleep in a cupboard under the stairs like Harry Potter (we don't even *have* a cupboard under the stairs) or sweep up cinders like Cinderella (our fireplaces are all gas and

Uncle Rick wired them so you can switch them on with a remote control, not that I'm allowed to).

I have my own room and everything. Aunt Catherine and her husband treat me ~~almost~~ just like I'm one of Uncle Rick's kids, so I don't have any right to complain.

Except that I do get sad sometimes that I'm not allowed to have a dog or cat (because Uncle Rick is allergic and Aunt Catherine doesn't want pet hair getting on her designer furniture or carpets).

It also kind of bums me out that Aunt Catherine and Uncle Rick's company, O'Toole Designs, has been hired to build a fancy new mall in a country

called Qalif, so we're moving there this summer. Even though I want to be adventurous, like my dad, I really don't want to move, because I'll miss Nishi.

Also, it's bad enough that I have to wear a skirt every day as part of my school uniform. Aunt Catherine says that in Qalif girls have to wear skirts *all the time*, and women have to cover their heads. It's the local custom.

I think I would prefer fighting mummies.

It also seems a little bit unfair to me that Aunt Catherine and Uncle Rick say I can't have my own computer like Sara and Justin (because there is not enough WiFi in the house to stretch to my room), or a mobile phone (Aunt Catherine says I can have one when I'm in high school, though, if I get good enough grades).

I guess I sort of do feel like I'm missing out a little, not texting or going online with my friends. Sara gets to, and she's only four months older than I am!

I definitely don't mind not having a TV in my room, though, like Justin and Sara. I want to be a wildlife illustrator when I grow up, so I don't have time to veg out in front of the TV, playing video games like Justin or watching reality shows like Sara. I have to practise my drawing. Wildlife illustrators are the ones who draw all the animals you see in books or on the Web or next to the exhibits when you go to the zoo.

People don't realize this, but baby kangaroos (called joeys) are born only two centimeters long, completely blind and hairless. They have to crawl into their mother's pouch, where they will stay for six to eight months until they are ready to come out and hop around.

Someone has to draw this because their kangaroo mom isn't going to let anyone inside the pouch to photograph it!

That's what wildlife illustrators do. Obviously I'm not a professional artist yet, but I took a free art test I found in the back of a magazine when I was in the dentist's office – the kind where they ask you to 'Draw Tippy the Turtle' as best you can – and sent it in. I have to admit, I never expected to hear back.

So I was more shocked than anyone when the art school called our house one day out of the blue and said they'd received my drawing of Tippy the Turtle and thought I had 'real talent'. They wanted to offer me a scholarship!

Of course they hung up as soon as Aunt Catherine told them I was twelve.

But still! From that day on, I knew I was going to be an artist. I mean, if I can get a scholarship at age twelve, I can definitely get one when I'm older.

Ms Dakota, my art teacher at school, agrees. She says I just have to keep practising, especially perspective (which is the art of drawing objects so that they appear multi-dimensional). Ms Dakota

showed me how to create a
vanishing point in the centre of
the page, then make sure all
the lines in my drawing met
there. It's super hard.

So hard that I have to admit I spend a lot of time
drawing kangaroos and cheetahs and our neighbour
Mrs Tucker's cats instead of practising my
perspective.

It's amazing how your whole life can change in
one day. Like the day I won the art scholarship
(even if I couldn't accept it). That was a really good
day, a day I went from being average to not-so-
average, in a good way, because someone thought I
was good at art.

Not like today, which is a *horrible* day.

I guess I should have known this day was going

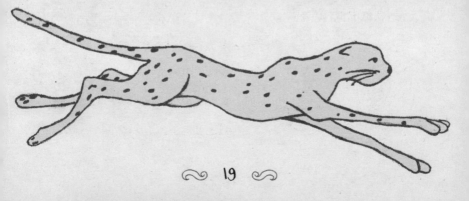

to be horrible the minute Mr Courtney handed out those 'Who Am I?' genetic family history worksheets in Bio.

What am I supposed to put under Father's Eye Colour – or Father's Mother's Eye Colour? Obviously I can write to Dad to find out, but by the time I get the answers, the worksheet will be overdue, and it's worth 25 per cent of our grade! (Although Mr Courtney says it's OK to leave some things blank. The twins, Netta and Quetta, don't know the biological information for their dad, either.)

But I really hate not knowing things.

Especially things like why Annabelle Jenkins would want to beat me up.

It makes no sense.

No sense at all.

Wednesday 6 May
2.52 p.m.
Social Studies Class

None of the girls I sit with at lunch can figure out why Annabelle wants to beat me up, either. Well, except maybe my step-cousin, Sara. But I don't agree it's 'because your nail polish doesn't match the colour of your shoes'.

'No one would beat someone up over that, Sara,' I said.

'Annabelle might.' Sara calmly sipped her diet soda. 'She's very fashion conscious.'

No one replied to this – mainly, I think, because we were all remembering how Sara used to eat lunch with Annabelle, until the day Sara made the mistake of wearing nail polish that didn't match her shoes, and Annabelle, mortally offended, banished her forever from the popular table.

Now Sara eats with us, the fun-but-not-always-fashionably-correct crowd.

Nishi said, 'Well, I still think you should tell a teacher, Olivia. It's not as if you've ever got in trouble before. A teacher is more likely to believe you over her anyway.'

'But what about Annabelle's dad?' Beth Chandler asked.

'What about him?' Nishi asked.

'I've seen his ads on TV,' one of the twins – either Netta or Quetta, I can't tell them apart, although I pretend I can – said. 'He's pretty famous.'

'For personal injury cases,' Nishi said. 'Like, if you've been in a car crash or something. Not for suing schools.'

'I wouldn't go up against Annabelle,' the other twin said. 'She rules this school.'

'Don't be dumb,' Nishi said. 'No one can rule a

school, especially not a sixth grader.'

'Annabelle Jenkins can,' Sara said. Obviously, Sara would know. 'She got invited to a seventh grader's party last weekend.'

I wanted to say, 'Not helping!' sarcastically to Sara, but she has no sense of humour when it comes to Annabelle.

Beth Chandler said I should fake a stomach ache and go to the nurse, then have the nurse call Aunt Catherine to come take me home before school ends.

But we all agreed I'd only be postponing the inevitable.

Finally one of the twins said, 'Why don't you tell Justin? Then if Annabelle comes near you he could defend you.'

This did not seem like a very good suggestion. I could see Justin sitting over with the other eighth-grade boys at a table by the cafeteria windows. They were playing with personal gaming devices, even though Dr Bushy, the principal, has said if you are caught with one during school hours it will be confiscated and you will lose a merit point.

I guess eighth graders don't care about losing merit points, though.

'Justin looks kind of busy,' I said.

'Whatever,' Nishi said. 'He's *family*. He *has* to help you.'

I've tried to explain to Nishi many times that, while it's true that Sara and Justin are my family, it's only because their dad married my aunt. They aren't actually blood relations. They're Aunt Catherine's step-kids, which makes them only my step-cousins.

I know this shouldn't mean we're any less close than if we were genetically cousins. Families can be made up of all different kinds of people, many of whom aren't related at all. Sometimes they aren't even the same species. Our neighbour Mrs Tucker considers her cats her children and likes to knit them tiny hats.

But the truth is I get the feeling sometimes that the fact that I'm not related to them by blood *super* matters to the O'Tooles.

'Don't do it,' Sara warned me, over her peanut

butter and jelly rice-cake sandwich (no one in the O'Toole household has coeliac disease or a wheat allergy like Beth Chandler, who cannot eat gluten or her throat closes up and she has to go to the hospital. Aunt Catherine just thinks gluten makes people overweight, so she doesn't keep any bread, pasta or cookies in the house). 'Remember what Justin said the first day of school.'

How could I forget it? The first day of school, Justin gave me a lecture. The lecture was about how, even though we'd be attending the same school, I wasn't supposed to talk to him, not even to ask for directions.

And I was most definitely *not* to mention to anyone the fact that at home Justin likes to sing to Taylor Swift on our household karaoke machine, or that he had cried at the end of *both* of the movies based on Princess Mia of Genovia's life.

'Oh, Sara, don't be mean,' Beth Chandler said. 'Justin will help her. Justin's so nice!'

Only someone who doesn't have to live in the same house with Justin would say this. Some of the girls think my step-cousin Justin is cute, but that is only because:

1. They don't have to live with him, and so have never smelled his extremely gross, stinky socks, like I have.

2. There are more girls than boys at Cranford Middle School, so some of the girls are ready to believe ANY boy is cute, even Justin.

'Uh,' I said. 'It's OK.'

'No, it isn't!' Beth Chandler said. 'Do it, Olivia.'

'Yes,' Nishi said. 'You should do it, Olivia.'

'Don't do it, Olivia,' Sara warned.

'It's an *emergency*,' one of the twins reminded her.

But Sara just shook her head and sucked on her diet soda.

'She'll be sorry,' she said.

But Nishi and Beth Chandler and the twins urged me to go ask Justin.

I should have listened to Sara.

But what other choice did I have? No one was coming up with a better idea, least of all me.

So I summoned up all my courage and went over to the table where Justin was sitting.

He was the one holding the gaming device. All the other boys were crowded around him, looking down at the little screen. They were saying things like, 'Go! Go!' and, 'Nuke him now.' It didn't actually seem like the best moment to interrupt, but, like Netta or Quetta had said, it was an emergency, after all.

'Um, Justin,' I said.

All the eighth-grade boys looked at me. All except Justin. He kept playing his game.

'Go away, Olivia,' he said.

'I'm really sorry to bother you,' I said. I was aware that Justin's friends had looked away, dismissing me as not worthy of their attention. Which was all right. There was only one person's attention I wanted anyway. 'But, um, I was wondering if I could talk to you in private?'

'I already told you,' Justin said, still not looking up from the game. 'Go away.'

'I know,' I said. 'But this is an emergency. You see, there's this girl, Annabelle Jenkins? You know her dad is your dad's business partner, right?'

'Lawyer,' Justin said, not looking at me.

'Um, sorry, right. His lawyer. So, she says she's going to give me a beat-down after school, but I don't know why. So I was wondering, if she tries to, will you, uh, help me?'

Justin made some kind of mistake in the game, and all the boys at his table went, 'Oh!' and a couple of them called him bad names. That's when Justin swung round to glare at me and said, *GO AWAY or Annabelle won't be the only one giving you a beat-down, Olivia Grace!'*

What Justin didn't know, though, was that Dr Bushy (the principal) was right there, doing his turn as cafeteria monitor.

He heard Justin yell at me. Dr Bushy doesn't like it when people yell in his cafeteria (or the hallways, where Justin and his friends frequently make fun of

sixth graders like me and Nishi for no reason), so he came right over.

'What's this? What's this?' Dr Bushy wanted to know. 'If you two can't get along nicely with each other, maybe I should give you both a demerit. Would that help?'

I nearly died. A demerit! After going the whole year without one!

Justin turned bright red and said, 'No, Dr Bushy. That would not help.'

'Now, that's more like it,' Dr Bushy said. 'What about you, Olivia? Would you like a demerit?'

'No, sir,' I said, swallowing. I couldn't see Annabelle anywhere, but I was sure she was watching. 'I wouldn't like one, either.'

'Good! Then go back to your seat!'

Then Dr Bushy left to go yell at some kids who were stuffing leftover pizza in the recycling bin instead of the compost bin.

I fled to my seat, practically crying.

'Oh my gosh!' Nishi said. 'Did Dr Bushy just give you a demerit?'

'I don't know,' I moaned, burying my face in my hands. 'I don't think so. But maybe!'

Netta and Quetta patted my back, murmuring soothing things, and Beth Chandler called Dr Bushy a name under her breath. Sara just said, 'Told you so,' about Justin. She sounded kind of smug about it.

Even though I wouldn't want one like Justin or Sara, sometimes I wish I had a sibling. I'm pretty sure if I did he or she would have my back in an emergency. Like now, as three o'clock grows closer with every jab of the minute hand.

Instead, I'm just going to have to face the fact that my first year of middle school?

It's probably going to be my last.

Wednesday 6 May
3.35 p.m.
Limousine

Yes, you read that right. I am writing this from the inside of a *limousine*.

It just goes to show that a lot can happen in an hour. You can go from having the worst day of your life to the best day (well, second best after the day I got the scholarship to art school).

I have to get all of this down or I feel like it might turn out all to have been a dream. Maybe I'll wake up in the hospital and the nurse will tell me I had a concussion in PE (except that they don't have contact sports in PE in my school any more because of litigation concerns) and imagined it all.

Except the buttery leather seat underneath me feels pretty real.

And the scent of the perfume of the *Royal Princess of Genovia* sitting beside me smells pretty real.

I think it's *all* real.

Maybe Dad is right, though, and writing it down will help it to make more sense. Like how keeping my class schedule taped to the inside of my organizer makes me feel better . . . Only this isn't a class schedule – it's my life! And I can't tape it into the front of an organizer because there *is* no organizer for life.

One thing is for sure: all the blank spaces on my 'Who Am I?' worksheet are getting filled in.

OK, deep breath . . .

So by the time the last bell of the day had rung, letting us know we were all free to go (some of us to get a beat-down courtesy of Annabelle Jenkins), my heart was jiggering around inside my chest like a baby joey inside its mom's pouch, only not at all cute.

I filled my backpack with all the books I might

need for homework for the next few nights (in case I ended up in the hospital) and headed to the courtyard where we're supposed to wait for our buses.

I saw a few people I recognized already in line for the bus we take home – including Sara and Justin. Justin was deeply involved in another round of whatever it was he'd been playing on his game device. Sara was pretending not to notice me.

But Nishi, Beth Chandler and the twins were standing nearby, looking nervously in the direction of the flagpole.

When I looked towards the flagpole, I saw why:

Annabelle was already there! She was waiting for me, just like she'd said she'd be.

I guess, deep down, I'd kind of been hoping she'd forgotten the whole thing. Girls like Annabelle, who are super busy being fashion forward and winning awards, might actually have a lot to do, and could possibly forget all the people they'd promised to beat up after school.

But apparently not Annabelle, since she was

staring right at me. She looked mad enough to beat up just about anyone, possibly even an eighth grader. If she'd been a microwave Hot Pocket (which I only get to eat when I go to Nishi's house, since they aren't gluten-free), I think steam would have been rising out of her – that's how mad she was.

At me. *Me*, who'd never done or said anything to her to make her that way!

The minute she saw me, she started storming towards me. My jiggering joey heart gave one last *thump-thump*, then seemed to die in my chest.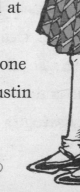

'Annabelle,' I said, in a final attempt to save myself. 'Can't we TALK about this? I don't know what I did to make you so mad at me, but—'

'Go on, Annabelle,' someone shouted from over near where Justin was standing. 'Get her!'

'Yeah, Annabelle! Get her!'

I looked over at Justin. His face was beet red as he bent over his gaming device, pretending he didn't notice what was going on.

But he knew. I knew he knew. Because next to him, some of his friends were grinning right at me. They knew what was going on and thought what was happening to me was funny.

But it wasn't funny. Because I could see all it was doing was getting Annabelle even more determined to carry out her threat.

'Really, Olivia?' she asked in a snotty voice when she got up to me. 'You *really* don't know what this is all about?'

'Uh, no,' I said, stalling for time.

There were teachers standing all around (except Ms Dakota, who leaves early on Wednesdays), and also parents there to pick up their kids.

But they clearly didn't know what was happening. To them it must have looked like Annabelle and I were simply standing there by the flagpole having a lovely little chat about, oh,

I don't know, nail polish or whatever.

Do grown-ups really not know that girls fight – really fight – with their fists? You would think there've been enough videos on the Internet about this by now that people would get the message.

Maybe everyone thinks, *Not* my *kid! Not at* our *school.*

Obviously none of these people have met Annabelle.

'I really don't know what this is about, Annabelle,' I said to her. 'We've always been friends. At least, I thought so.'

'Well, you thought wrong,' Annabelle said, loudly enough so that all her smirking friends could hear (but none of the teachers or parents, of course). 'Because I'm not friends with liars.'

'What?' This was the *last* thing I ever expected her to say. 'I never lied to you, Annabelle—'

'Oh yeah? Well, how about the lie I heard you said at Netta and Quetta's sleepover last weekend, that your father is some kind of famous archaeologist like Indiana Jones?'

I felt myself blushing. Contrary to popular opinion, black people *can* blush, and even get sunburned (and skin cancer from the sun if we don't put on sunscreen). It's just that because our skin is darker coloured it doesn't show as much.

'OK,' I said. 'Well, that may have been a slight exaggeration—'

'She never said he was *exactly* like Indiana Jones, Annabelle,' Nishi said, coming to my defence.

'Because he isn't,' Annabelle scoffed. 'Her dad is *nothing* like Indiana Jones. I know because I heard my dad talking to her uncle, and the truth is her dad is actually a prince. *The Prince of Genovia*, to be exact!'

I wasn't the only one who thought Annabelle had started spewing crazy gibberish. All the other kids did too, at least judging from the way they started laughing.

'Yeah, right,' I heard one of the boys say. A few of them who were disappointed the fight hadn't started yet yelled, 'Kick her butt, Annabelle!'

Obviously, what Annabelle was saying was not

true, and it was certainly no reason to want to beat me up.

But I still felt obliged to defend myself, and of course keep my butt from getting kicked.

'Annabelle,' I said. 'That's crazy.'

'Are you calling my dad crazy?' she demanded, reaching out to give my shoulder a one-handed shove, like she had earlier in the day, in the hallway.

'No, of course not,' I said, managing to keep my balance this time. 'I'm just saying your dad's been misinformed. If my father were the Prince of Genovia, someone would have told me.'

I glanced over at my step-cousins. Justin wore an expression that clearly stated, 'Her dad? A prince? Yeah, right!' while Sara merely looked confused.

'See?' I said to Annabelle.

She rolled her eyes.

'How could they tell you?' she demanded. 'Your mother never wanted anyone to know, not even you. She was afraid you'd get kidnapped or something stupid like that. Plus she said she wanted you to be raised like a normal kid. Like *you* could ever be normal!'

Annabelle let out another mocking laugh, then pushed me again.

But this time I barely noticed, because suddenly some things were starting to make sense: like how Aunt Catherine never wanted to talk about my dad.

And how I never got to go visit him on weekends or during the summer, like other kids.

And how the support cheques he sent for me were pretty big (for an archaeologist) but Aunt Catherine and Uncle Rick wouldn't let me have my own mobile phone or computer.

That's because if they had, and I'd had unlimited time on the Internet, I might have looked up stuff about my dad, and discovered . . .

'Wait a minute,' I burst out. 'That *can't* be true. There's no way my dad is the Prince of Genovia. Because that would make *me* a—'

'*Princess?*' Annabelle sneered.

Everyone in the courtyard gasped.

'No,' I cried, staggering back. 'No *way*.'

'Well, that's what you are, *Princess Olivia*. Should we all curtsy and bow down to you now? Where's your tiara, Your Royal Highness? Did you forget it, back at the *palace*?'

'No!' I couldn't believe this was happening. 'No!'

'Oh, what's the matter, Your Highness?' Annabelle sneered. 'Princess gonna cry?'

'No!' Although the truth was I did feel a little bit like crying. Because I realized it was true. It was all true. It had to be. In a weird way, it kind of made sense.

Fortunately Nishi came to my defence once more.

'Stop it, Annabelle,' she cried. 'Olivia isn't a princess!'

'Uh, yes, she is,' Annabelle said. 'But it doesn't matter, because I'm still going to kick her butt.'

That's when she hurled herself towards me, and everyone around us – except my friends, of course – suddenly started screaming, 'FIGHT! FIGHT! FIGHT!'

I knew then that I was going to die.

I've seen people fight in movies and on TV. It looks pretty easy when you're watching a trained actor or stunt person do it.

But when a *real live person* who is not a trained actor but the most popular girl in your school (don't ask me why, because Annabelle is actually very mean) who is also a trained gymnast jumps you, then gets hold of one of your braids and starts pulling on it *very hard*, it is not easy to fight back.

I thought I was a complete goner until right at that very moment a woman's voice rang out, clear as a bell, from across the courtyard.

'Olivia?' the voice called. 'Olivia Grace Harrison!'

Startled, I turned to look – as much as I could with Annabelle hanging so tightly on to my braid – and saw the most amazing sight I had ever seen in my life:

Her Royal Highness, Princess Mia Thermopolis of Genovia.

Wednesday 6 May
4.15 p.m.
Still in the Royal Limousine

Sorry, I got interrupted there. It turns out when you're a princess you get all the soda you want to drink from the limo mini-bar.

FOR FREE!

Also crisps and cookies.

I know that's a weird thing to be writing about at a time like this – and also that they're only giving these things to me because I mentioned that Aunt Catherine never lets me have soda with sugar in it, or crisps and cookies.

But it's so nice!

I just hope they aren't doing it because they feel sorry for me. That would be the *worst*. I hate it when people feel sorry for me (because I'm half an orphan, etc.).

Where was I? Oh, yes, back in the courtyard.

I don't have to explain how I recognized her. Everyone knows what Princess Mia looks like. She's had movies made about her, and books written based on her diaries, and was just recently on the cover of *People* magazine, and she was also in *Us Weekly*'s 'Stars: They're Just Like Us' section, buying toilet paper (even though it's hard to imagine a princess using the bathroom).

It was also easy to recognize her because she was

standing in front of this huge black stretch limousine with little flags on it, and there was this man next to her who was almost as huge as the limo (only not black, though he was dressed in a black suit and had on black sunglasses, and he was glaring very meanly right at Annabelle).

It wasn't hard to tell that the man was Princess Mia's bodyguard.

'Olivia?' Princess Mia called, waving as if she wasn't sure I'd seen her.

But I'd seen her all right, because who could miss her, standing there in this cream-coloured coat with a long floaty red scarf and matching red high-heel shoes?

Annabelle had seen her too. I could tell because

Annabelle froze with her hand right there on my braid.

Every other kid in the entire courtyard froze too. Most of the adults did, as well, including Ms Feinstein, the car-park attendant, who'd been blowing her whistle at the buses a minute before. They all just stood there, frozen, staring at Princess Mia of Genovia and her long red scarf, floating in the spring breeze.

'Um,' I said to Annabelle, breaking the sudden silence. 'I think that lady over there with the limo wants to talk to me.'

I heard Annabelle swallow, hard. It might have been my imagination, but she looked a little scared, especially at the sight of Princess Mia's frowning bodyguard. Even my step-cousin Justin and all his friends were staring at the bodyguard. No one was yelling FIGHT FIGHT FIGHT any more. Instead, there was dead silence in the courtyard. Even the bus engines had stopped.

'OK,' Annabelle whispered, and dropped my braid.

When Princess Mia reached us, I brushed off my uniform, which was a little dusty from my nearly being killed, and said, 'Hi, yes, that's me. I'm Olivia.'

'Oh,' Princess Mia said, smiling at me. Up close, she looked even more like she does on TV. I know that sounds strange, but that's what it was like. Seeing someone from TV, only without the TV box around her. She looked very beautiful and nice.

But that also could have been because she was like an angel who had come to rescue me from being killed by Annabelle Jenkins.

'Hello. I'm Mia Thermopolis,' she went on. 'Your aunt Catherine said it would be all right for me to pick you up from school today.'

I didn't know what to say to that. Why would

Aunt Catherine send the princess of Genovia to pick me up from school? That made no sense at all, but it was totally OK by me.

As if in answer to my silent question, Princess Mia said, 'Oh, here's a note from your aunt,' and handed me a sheet of paper.

I could tell everyone was watching me as I unfolded the note from Aunt Catherine. Some of them weren't only watching me – they were filming me on their phone cameras. No one had ever filmed me before in my life except for Sara, the time she'd snuck into my room and stuck my hand in a bowl of warm water while I slept to see if I would wet my pants (to her disappointment, I did not).

All the filming was making me uncomfortable. I'm obviously not the kind of girl people film. I'm an artist! No one makes TV shows called *America's Top Artist* or *Drawing with the Stars*! Drawing isn't the most exciting thing to watch, although of course it's nice to look at what someone's drawn after they're done drawing it.

The note my aunt had signed was written on

royal Genovian stationery, and had a gold crown embossed at the top. A lot of the writing was hard to understand, but basically it said that Princess Amelia 'Mia' Mignonette Grimaldi Thermopolis Renaldo had permission to transport me to any destination of my choosing.

Any destination of my choosing?

No one had ever taken me to a destination of my own choosing before! If they had, I'd have chosen to go to Cheesecake Factory EVERY SINGLE TIME. We never get to go to Cheesecake Factory, because the O"Tooles like Olive Garden for its many gluten-free options.

I carefully folded the note and put it in my backpack so I wouldn't lose it. It was definitely something I wanted to keep forever, like all the letters from my dad.

'So, would you like to come with me?' Princess Mia asked.

'Thank you,' I said, trying to sound as dignified as possible, since I could tell everyone was listening. 'I'd like that very much.'

'Great,' Princess Mia said, smiling. 'Let's go.'

I know it's not polite to gloat, but it felt pretty good to walk across the courtyard to my WAITING LIMO while Annabelle had to wait for her BUS to take her home, especially after she'd tried to beat me up for no reason other than the fact that she seems to think I'm a princess.

(Which is apparently a fact.)

It felt even better when Annabelle ran after us, going, 'Excuse me? Excuse me, but is it true you're Olivia's sister?' to Princess Mia in a very snotty voice.

Sister?

Of everything that's happened so far, this may have been the best:

Princess Mia looked at Annabelle and was like, 'Who *are* you?'

This completely shocked Annabelle, because Annabelle thinks everyone knows who she is, since she's won so many gymnastics medals, etc.

But the truth is, I'm pretty sure outside of

Cranbrook Middle School (and possibly even outside of the sixth grade of Cranbrook Middle School) *no one* knows who Annabelle Jenkins is.

Poor Annabelle. And I thought *I* was having a bad day!

Annabelle sputtered, 'I-I-I'm Annabelle Jenkins! My father is Bill Jenkins, Olivia's step-uncle's lawyer. He's the highest-rated personal injury lawyer in all of Cranbrook, New Jersey. And *he* says that—'

'Well, I'm sorry, Annabelle,' Princess Mia said, in a voice like silk, 'but this is a private family matter. I'm afraid I don't have time to chat today. Goodbye.'

Private family matter! Without exactly admitting it, Princess Mia had just confirmed everything Annabelle had said back by the flagpole.

I *am* a princess! And she *is* my sister!

If I could have drawn the look on Annabelle's face at that moment, it would have resembled a smiley with blank eyes and a surprised *O* for a mouth, exactly like this:

Then Princess Mia made one little gesture – she took my hand – and suddenly everyone went completely bananas. They came rushing towards us, yelling, 'Olivia, Olivia, can I get a selfie with you?'

In the entire time I've gone to school in Cranbrook, no one has ever asked for a selfie with me, except Nishi, who has selfies with me all over her social media pages, only of course I can't see them because Aunt Catherine won't let me have any social media pages.

Now I know why.

But then Princess Mia's bodyguard (who I have now learned is named Lars) said, 'NO!' to everyone in a pretty scary voice. He even yelled at Dr Bushy, who wanted a selfie with me and Princess Mia, and was even pushier than everyone else about it (and since Dr Bushy has such a large stomach he managed to push his way through the crowd more quickly than everyone else too, using his belly as a kind of battering ram).

He looked pretty shocked when Lars yelled at him – probably because Dr Bushy is the one who does most of the yelling (and handing out of demerits) around CMS. After Lars yelled at him, Dr Bushy just stood there in the middle of the car park, still holding his mobile phone, looking confused.

And then the next thing I knew, *my sister* and I were getting into the limo and the door was slamming behind us and all the kids had started banging on the windows screaming, 'Olivia! Olivia, wait!' because they hadn't got a photo, and *my sister* looked a bit startled and asked, 'Oh dear, what's happening?'

'Oh, nothing,' I told her. 'They're just excited. Not many celebrities visit Cranbrook Middle

School. Actually, you're the first.'

This didn't make her look very relieved, especially after the chauffeur – there is a chauffeur! He drives the limo. His name is Francois – had to blow the horn very loudly to get all the kids to move out of the way so we could drive out of the car park and on to the road.

The last thing I saw as I looked out of the window was Nishi, standing on the sidewalk a little away from the crowd, waving to me.

I waved back, but I don't know if she could see me, because the windows of the limo are tinted so that the people inside can see out, but people outside can't see in.

Meanwhile Princess Mia kept apologizing.

'I'm so sorry, Olivia, but I had no idea I even *had* a sister until a few days ago. And you certainly shouldn't have found out *this* way that you're – that we're—'

I could tell that she was really uncomfortable – which was kind of funny: a princess, being uncomfortable around *me*.

That's the thing about royalty, though: they have a hard job to do. They have to try to set a good example and make everyone feel happy, while also being brave and beautiful and stuff.

I know all this because Nishi loves princess movies, so whenever I go to her house she makes me watch them with her (not that it's a huge sacrifice).

Nishi doesn't care that Annabelle started saying, as long ago as first grade, that princess movies are for babies. Nishi says you like what you like, so who cares what other people think?

That's why I actually felt a little bad for Princess Mia. In movies, princesses are always getting kidnapped and then put into dungeons until they use their magical powers (or ray guns) to escape.

But, in real life, princesses don't have magical powers or ray guns. All they have are their brains (and bodyguards and limousines, of course), which they're supposed to use to help make the world a better place. None of it's as easy as it looks, especially to people like Annabelle, who think all princesses do is sit around in nice clothes, which isn't true at all.

'It's OK,' I said. 'Annabelle already told me. Just not in a very nice way. She can be a bit of a snob.'

'That's what I'm so sorry about,' Princess Mia said, looking upset. 'Because you haven't done anything wrong!'

'I know. My mom – and dad – were only trying to protect me. And I can see why, after all that out there.' I jerked my thumb in the direction of CMS.

Princess Mia exchanged glances with some other women who were also in the limo – I think they were ladies-in-waiting – and said, 'Yes. I'm sorry about that too. I should have known better, and stayed in the limo. I'm so sorry—'

I shook my head. It was still funny that a princess was apologizing so much to *me*. 'It's OK. So is it really true?'

'That we're sisters? Yes, of course it's really true.'

'No, that you'll take me to any destination of my choosing?'

Princess Mia looked a little more relaxed, which was what I wanted. She seemed very tense and worried. More tense and worried than me! And that's saying a lot, considering the day I'd had so far.

'Yes,' she said, with a laugh. 'That's really true too. Why? Is there somewhere you really want to go?'

I couldn't believe she didn't know.

'Yes!' I cried. 'To meet my dad!'

Princess Mia smiled. 'I was hoping you'd say that.'

Wednesday 6 May
4.45 p.m.
Limousine

I'M GOING TO MEET MY DAD.
IN NEW YORK CITY.

I'm sorry to write it so big, but I'm very, very excited.

We should be there in a little over an hour. Cranbrook, New Jersey, is only sixty-four miles from New York City, but I've never been there. Nishi has been there lots of times with her family, and Aunt Catherine and Uncle Rick go there a lot too – to Broadway shows and baseball games and fancy restaurants and stuff.

But not me. I've always ended up having to stay home with Mrs Tucker, our neighbour who owns the cats, or with Nishi, because Aunt Catherine says the city is too dirty and dangerous for children, even though I'm not exactly a child and they take Sara all the time, which I've always thought was a little weird since she's not that much older than I am.

But now I am starting to realize that it probably had something to do with my being a princess.

Aunt Catherine never put it that way, though, of course. She always said, 'Oh, Olivia, the city is so dirty,' and, 'You'd just have been bored at the show we went to.'

I guess my mom was pretty serious about keeping this whole princess thing a secret. She made my dad promise not to tell *anyone*, not even his own mom (who is my grandma. Mia says she likes to be called Grandmère, which is French for grandmother).

'I can't believe he didn't tell *me*,' Princess Mia keeps saying. 'I wish I'd known sooner, because I've always wanted a sister.'

'Me too!'

The one thing I've always wanted, and it's come true!

And it turns out Princess Mia and I have a lot in common:

She has a diary too. She saw me writing in this notebook and asked if I was doing homework and I said no, that my dad said to write down my feelings when I was getting overwhelmed.

That's when Mia got a funny look on her face and said, 'Hmmm, I think I know where he got that idea.'

'Where?' I asked, surprised.

'My mom told me to do the same thing when I was about your age.'

'Really?' I asked.

'Yes,' she said, and smiled. 'So what else do you like to do, besides write in your diary?'

'I like to draw.' I showed her a couple of my wildlife illustrations.

'Wow, those are really good! You must have inherited that talent from your mom, because I can't draw at all.'

'Oh, that's not true,' I assured her. 'My art teacher, Ms Dakota, says anyone can learn to draw if they practise a little every day. The thing she wants me to practise right now is perspective. She says it's easy with practice. But even though I've been practising and practising, I still can't seem to get it right.'

Princess Mia glanced again at my drawings. 'Your perspective looks good to me. Better than mine, that's for sure.'

'Aw,' I said, feeling myself blush. 'Not really.'

She smiled. 'The first thing you'll have to learn, Olivia, if you're going to get this princess thing right, is how to take a compliment. When someone says something nice to you, don't put yourself down. Just say "thank you". Try it.'

I blushed harder. 'Thank you.'

'You're welcome,' she said, laughing. 'See, that wasn't so hard, was it? It's like what your art teacher said about perspective. The more you practise, the easier it will get.'

I frowned. 'I never thought of it that way.'

I'd only said 'Not really' because I didn't want to seem like a snob.

But I guess saying 'thank you' when someone pays you a compliment doesn't sound snobby. It's the polite thing to do.

So then, to change the subject, I showed Princess Mia my 'Who Am I?' worksheet (not that I like to do homework, of course, but it's due tomorrow), and she started to help me fill it out, saying she'd be happy to answer any questions I had about our Genovian ancestry . . .

Except then she got a call on her mobile phone that she said she was sorry she had to take.

I said I understood. Being a princess really is hard work.

The thing is, I have some questions I don't think Princess Mia can answer, such as:

If my mom was so serious about me not knowing my royal heritage, why did she name me after so many Genovian princesses?

Is it for the same reason Aunt Catherine said it was my mother's 'dream' that I learned to speak

French, and why she makes me take it in school, even though everyone else takes Spanish? French is the language they speak in Genovia.

I can't help thinking it's because my mom meant to tell me the truth some day, and go with me to Genovia. She just died before she ever got the chance.

Her making me learn French is already doing me some good, though. I don't mean to be eavesdropping, but I can understand some of what Princess Mia has been saying on her mobile phone (in French).

I should probably interrupt and mention that I take French. But I don't want to be rude. Also, it's kind of interesting.

One of the ladies-in-waiting (Tina) let me borrow her extra mobile phone (when you're royal I guess you're so rich you have two).

'So you can play games and won't be bored during the drive,' she said kindly, but I think it's more so that they can talk amongst themselves.

Instead of playing games I'm going to text Nishi (she taught me how in case I ever got my own phone, and obviously I have her number memorized, since I can only ever call her from the house phone in the kitchen).

Nishi is never going to believe any of this!

< NishiGirl   **Olivia >**

> Hi, Nish, it's me, Olivia! I'm using the phone of one of the royal ladies-in-waiting. ;-)

OMG I'm so glad u r OK! I've been so worried! The police came after u left!

> The police? Why? To arrest Annabelle? HA HA HA.

Ha, no, though they should have. I couldn't believe it when she jumped u!

> Thanks for having my back.

Any time. The police came because no one would get on their buses!

< NishiGirl   Olivia >

Really???

Really! Dr Bushy was so mad. I think he called them, but Quetta says Annabelle did. She's so immature. So is it true????

Is what true?

What Annabelle said: That u r a princess!!!!!!

Uh. Yes.

How can u be so calm about it????

I'm not, believe me! I'm already getting princess lessons!

Where???

The limo!

What's it like?????

< NishiGirl   Olivia >

It's cool. I get all the crisps and soda I want! And the ceiling lights up all pink and purple and green when you press a button.

Cool!

I know. But my sister said to please stop pressing it because it was making her want to throw up.

What's ur sister like???

She's super nice. But I don't think she's used to 12 year olds. She asked me if I want to go to the American Girl doll store for tea!

HA HA HA!!!!! Did u tell her u don't have an American Girl doll and that u r 12 not 7?

No! These people are ROYAL. I'm trying to be polite.

I would totally go!!!

I know u would. U r the one who had lunch at Disney World at the Beauty and the Beast castle last Christmas and got ur picture taken with the Beast.

IT'S MY PROFILE PHOTO!!!

I know. Listen Nishi, my sister is on her phone and I can't understand everything she's saying because it's in French, but I think I heard her say the word 'stole'.

U better stop eating so many crisps.

Not about me! I think it was about Aunt Catherine and Uncle Rick!

i TOLD u it was strange that they own 2 Ferraris. Most people don't even own 1.

They aren't car thieves!

How do u know? They have a lot of tools.

< NishiGirl   Olivia >

> The tools are because they own a home design and construction company!

> I knew there was something weird about u moving to a place where everyone has to cover their faces! They're on the run!

I love Nishi, but she can be so dramatic sometimes. I think it's from living with her grandmother, who watches a lot of Bollywood movies, which are great but not very realistic. I have never seen a whole room of people get up and do the same dance at the same time.

> The men in Qalif don't have to cover their faces, Nishi, only the women. Just forget I mentioned it.

> OK, but don't say I didn't warn u. Where r u going now? To have tea at the American Doll cafe?

> Ha ha. No. To meet my dad! IN NEW YORK CITY!

< NishiGirl   Olivia >

☺☺☺☺☺☺☺☺ !!!!!!!!!!!!!!
I AM SO HAPPY FOR U!!!!

I know! I'M FINALLY GOING TO MEET MY DAD!!!!

OMG, this is so cool. It is the coolest
thing ever. Can I tell everyone?

I think everyone already knows about the princess thing.

No, the part about ur dad. And they don't know
the princess part for real. U just confirmed it!

Well, I think Princess Mia confirmed it when she showed
up at school in a limo, but OK, I guess u can tell them.

YAY!!!!! I can't wait to see Annabelle's
face tomorrow when she hears!

Why?

Because now u r officially a princess!
And she's going to be sick with jealousy!

> Nishi, Annabelle hates princesses, remember? She's NOT jealous of me.

Duh! She hates princesses because she knows she'll never be one, not even on the inside. People who r that snobby and mean r always super insecure. That's why she wanted to beat u up.

> Uh, I'm pretty sure that's not why . . .

Trust me, that's why. I'm a princess expert. I know a hater when I see one.

I know Nishi likes to think she's a princess expert, but she's wrong. Annabelle Jenkins, the most popular girl in the sixth grade at Cranford Middle School, will never be jealous of me—

Uh-oh . . .

We're here.

Wednesday 6 May
6.30 p.m.
The Plaza Hotel

When my dad isn't in Genovia, being the prince, he stays at the Plaza Hotel on Fifth Avenue, which Aunt Catherine once told me has the most expensive apartments in all of New York, possibly the world.

I believe it! Everything here is super elegant. In fact, I feel pretty underdressed in my school uniform, especially my hideous pleated skirt, which is probably going to be famous now because so many people took photos of me in it when I got out of the limo.

That's because *someone* posted pictures online of

me with Princess Mia in front of Cranford Middle School, and tagged her as my sister!

Hmmm, I wonder who that *someone* could have been . . . no, I'm being sarcastic. I'm pretty sure it was Annabelle, seeing how much she hates me.

Anyway, that tipped off the media, and every single last one of them (it seemed) showed up outside the Plaza.

'This is going to be bad,' Princess Mia said as we pulled up in front of the red carpet leading to the front doors of the hotel.

I had to agree with her. I've never in my WHOLE LIFE seen as many people holding cameras as were waiting for us in front of that hotel! At first I thought it must have been for some sort of movie premiere or something . . .

But, when the limo stopped, and a man in a green uniform with gold braid on it came up to the door of the limo and opened it, and I heard all the people with cameras yelling *my* name, I knew: It wasn't a movie premiere. Those people were there for me. ME!

And they weren't just yelling my name, either, but a lot of questions, some of them not very nice (or true), like:

1. How did I feel about having been 'abandoned' by my rich white dad?

2. Did I think it was because I was black?

3. Was I upset that my parents never got married?

4. Who was I going to sue first?

5. What was I going to do now that I was a princess, go to Disneyland? (OK, this question was kind of funny. Not *all* the questions were mean.)

Princess Mia heard the rude questions too. I could tell because she looked angry. Her mouth got very small and her eyebrows slanted down.

'Uh,' I said, looking out at all the reporters. 'Maybe we should come back some other time.'

'No,' Princess Mia said, reaching out to straighten my school tie. 'It's always going to be like this. I'm afraid you're just going to have to get used to it. You don't have to answer them if you don't want to. In fact, I recommend that you don't. Just smile and wave.'

'Smile and wave?' I was a little bit shocked. I didn't think people asking things like that – things that were so rude, and weren't in the least bit true – deserved to be smiled at, much less waved to. 'Really?'

'Really.' She showed me how to smile very big, and wave using only my hand, not my whole arm, because it's less tiring. 'Yes, that's right,' she said when I tried it. 'Then smile like this.' She pasted a giant smile on her face.

I tried it, though it felt very fake. I didn't see how anyone could possibly believe it was a real smile. 'Like this?'

'Bigger,' she said, still waving and smiling, but

not moving her lips at all when she spoke. 'There, you've got it. Perfect. You're a natual.'

I said I didn't *feel* like a natural, so Princess Mia let me practise another minute or so. We didn't have anyone to practise smiling and waving to inside the limo except Francois and Lars, since we'd dropped the ladies-in-waiting off at their apartments, so we smiled and waved to them. Lars looked the most impressed, and offered a few other instructions.

'Ready?' he finally asked, and Princess Mia looked at me.

I shrugged, even though my stomach was filled with nervous butterflies, and slipped on my backpack, wishing it was a magic shield like some of the warrior princesses in Nishi's movies have. But there are no magic shields. 'I guess so.'

'Good,' Lars said. 'One, two, *three*.'

On 'three' we got out of the limo and hurried across the red carpet and up the steps to the hotel's front door. The truth was so many flashbulbs were going off I could hardly see where I was walking. If it hadn't been for Princess Mia's hand round my arm, I would have tripped and fallen flat on my face.

Fortunately the reporters were being held back by the doormen (and even some police officers). Everyone was shouting, 'Princess Olivia! Princess Olivia! Over here!' I couldn't hear anything else.

I almost looked, even though Lars had said not to. His instructions in the limo were:

1. Don't look.

2. Don't answer anyone's questions.

3. Don't accept any gifts anyone might try to give you.

4. Even if you see your best friend standing there in the crowd, don't go up to her.

I'd thought about Nishi and how much I was missing her (even though we'd just been texting) and had asked him why.

'Because then everyone will start crowding her

in order to touch you, and there'll be a stampede, and the barricade will fall down, and your friend will get trampled,' he'd said. 'If you want to see your friend get trampled, that's fine.'

'Uh . . . I don't, thanks,' I'd said.

'If your friend really wants to see you, the safest thing for her to do is schedule an appointment.'

I guess this is how it is to be a princess. People ask you rude questions and expect you to answer. You can't hop on your bike and go over to your friend's house any more or you'll be mobbed (or kidnapped). Instead, you have to 'schedule an appointment' to see each other.

Still, I really wanted to be able to share what was happening with Nishi (despite the mean questions).

So when I got to the top of the steps, I turned round and snapped a quick pic of all the people yelling.

I can't wait to see what Nishi says when I send it to her.

The inside of the Plaza Hotel is the fanciest place I've ever been in my LIFE. The ceilings are probably about a hundred feet high, and the chandeliers are made out of real crystals and GOLD. Probably one hundred per cent. I couldn't stop staring at everything. I felt so out of place! There was even a lady playing a HARP in a room that Princess Mia (I still feel weird calling her my sister) told me is called the Palm Court.

'You're lucky we're not going there,' she said on our way to the elevators. 'They make you eat egg salad sandwiches.'

'I like egg salad sandwiches,' I said. 'I like any kind of sandwiches, as long as they have gluten.'

'Oh,' she said. 'Well, then we'll go there later and you can have all the egg salad sandwiches you want.'

Except for the mean reporters, it's like I've died and gone to heaven.

On the elevator there was a man whose job it is *just to work the elevator*. He rides in it up and down all day, so the rich people don't have to tire themselves out, pushing all the buttons.

I bet he gets carsick. I looked around, but I didn't see any throw-up. They probably take the bucket away when no one is looking.

'Hello, Lyle,' Princess Mia said to the elevator man. 'Lyle, I'd like you to meet my sister, Olivia.'

'Hello, Princess Olivia,' Lyle said. He nodded as he pushed the button that said 'PE'. At first I thought, Why would they be taking me to do physical education? School was out hours ago! Then I realized PE had to stand for something else.

'Hope you have a nice visit,' Lyle said.

'Thanks,' I said politely. 'I hope I will too.'

The elevator ride to PE took a long time and, when the doors opened, there was no sign of a gymnasium. Instead, we were in a red-carpeted hallway with white walls trimmed in gold. A sign on the wall said in elegant gold script *PENTHOUSE EAST*. So *that's* what PE stood for. The east penthouse!

I had never been in a penthouse before, but I knew from all the TV I'd seen at Nishi's house that it was the fanciest apartment in the building. Also, it was on the top floor of the building, so that meant it was the most expensive. Obviously, princes are very rich, from having saved all their family money for many hundreds of years, which is another reason it made me so mad that those reporters downstairs had asked about my dad 'abandoning' me, when actually he'd sent me large cheques (and personal letters) every month, and it had been my mother who'd requested I not be told of my royal heritage.

Then, as we walked down the long, hushed hallway, which was filled with tall vases of real live white roses, I noticed that a door was open at the end of the hallway, and standing in the doorway was an old white lady I recognized from some of the same magazines in which I'd seen Princess Mia. But I'd never bothered to read anything about her because she looked so boring.

Except that Princess Mia looked pretty scared of her. She was standing up straighter and holding her bag tighter.

'So this is she?' the old lady asked, before we'd got all the way down the hallway.

'This is she, Grandmère,' Princess Mia said in a very polite voice.

I couldn't believe it! *This* was
my grandmother, Dowager Princess
Clarisse Renaldo? She looked
completely unlike any grandma I've
ever seen! She wasn't warm and
cuddly like Nishi's grandma, who

loves to cook and tell stories about life back in India, where Nishi's family comes from.

My dad's mom is tall and skinny and was dressed in a dark purple suit with even *darker* purple fur on the cuffs of her sleeves (and I'm pretty sure it wasn't fake fur, which we learned in school isn't very environmentally conscious), and her fingernails were long and pointy and her long white hair was piled up on top of her head in a big bun.

Also, I'm not sure but I think she might have drawn her eyebrows on with a black pencil and she had on about a million giant rings that I think were real diamonds and rubies and pearls and emeralds. In fact I *know* they were, because she's a princess!

Mia poked me in the back and suddenly I remembered what she'd taught me in the car to do and say when I met my grandmother.

'It's so nice to meet you, Grandmoth– is that a miniature *poodle*?'

I hadn't meant to say that last part, but I couldn't help it! All of a sudden as I was curtsying I saw this little white powder puff with a tiny black nose peeking out from around Grandmère's feet.

'I love poodles!' I cried. 'They're the most intelligent breed of dog. And they're also very excellent swimmers.'

I didn't mean to start yelling everything I know about dogs in front of my new royal grandmother.

But I just really, really like dogs, almost as much as I love kangaroos. Aunt Catherine would never let us have one (not a kangaroo, of course, but a dog or a cat or even a guinea pig).

'Yes,' my grandmother said very stiffly. 'Poodles *are* very intelligent, aren't they? Did you know they were used as defence dogs on the home front in World War II?'

'Yes,' I said. 'I've read all about them. They also don't shed.' I had tried this argument many times on Aunt Catherine in order to convince her to let us get a poodle, but it had never worked.

'Interesting. My *other* granddaughter only likes cats.'

Grandmère looked at my sister, who said, 'I don't

only like cats. I've only ever *had* a cat. Grandmère, could we come in now . . . ?'

Grandmère opened the door to let us in, and I couldn't believe what I found inside.

Besides the floors being white marble, streaked with black, like in a museum, there were antiques all over the place! I don't mean just any antiques, like fancy paintings on the walls – though there were lots of those, of old-timey sailing ships and fruit and pretty ladies in wigs, with huge gold frames around them – but also:

1. An actual mummified hawk in an Egyptian sarcophagus.

2. Tusks from narwhals, which are practically extinct now, and I'm pretty sure illegal to own outside of museums.

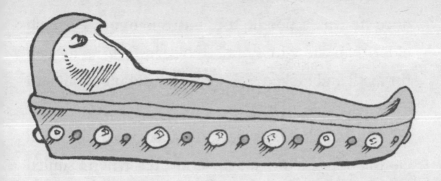

3. A white grand piano.

4. A suit of armour.

Even the furniture you're allowed to sit on is antique and way fancier than anything Aunt Catherine owns, and she gets all her furniture directly from designers' showrooms in Manhattan.

I was staring at the view of Central Park outside the huge, floor-to-ceiling windows – which are really doors, leading out to a huge balcony – not being able to believe my grandma lived in a building so chic that it has doormen *and* an elevator attendant, when *another* dog came running into the room from another part of the apartment. I knew at once he was a poodle too, but this one was much older than the white one, so old, in fact, he had no fur at all and looked like a wrinkly old man, but still quite adorable, of course.

The old dog was barking and growling like a guard dog as he hurried up to me, but when I smiled and squatted down to be eye level with him, he stopped dead in his tracks and stared at me.

'Well, hello,' I said. It was hard not to laugh at such a little dog who clearly thought he was so ferocious.

That's when he put his paws on my knees and started licking my face, his little tail wagging so fast it was a blur.

'Hi,' I said, grabbing him and scooping him up in my arms so he could kiss me more. 'How are you?' Even though he was so wrinkly and naked without his fur, he was still quite soft and warm.

'Rommel?' Grandma sounded shocked. 'Whatever is the matter with that dog?'

'Nothing's the matter with him,' I said.

'He's never let *anyone* pick him up like that.'

'Oh, I'm sorry.'

I started to put Rommel down, but Grandma said, 'No, no, never mind. If he likes you, he likes you. Would you like a cocktail?'

'Grandmère,' I heard my sister call from the next room. *'She's twelve.'*

'I meant an aperitif, of course.'

Has there ever been a luckier girl than me in all the world? I've found out I have:

1. A sister

2. A grandmother

3. And two adopted poodles

all in one day!

Just when I thought things couldn't get better, I was running around after Snowball (that's the girl poodle, who still has her fur. Grandma said I could name her, so I picked Snowball) and I went past this one room filled with books and there was a bald white man standing there on his mobile phone and I knew – I just knew – he was my dad.

(Well, also because I'd seen photos of the prince of Genovia in the same magazines I'd seen Princess Mia and Grandma, and the man at the desk looked exactly like the photos. Only less mean, somehow, because he'd shaved off his moustache.)

When he saw me, he got a strange expression on his face and said, 'Barry, I'm going to have to call you back,' and put his phone in his pocket and asked, 'Olivia?'

I didn't even stop to think. Because when you see your father for the first time in your whole life, you don't have to think. You just run over to where he's standing and throw your arms around him and hug him, even though of course, being a prince, he's wearing military medals.

'Oof,' he said, I guess because I'd buried my head in his stomach pretty hard.

But he hugged me back, saying, 'It's very good to meet you at last.'

'You have no idea.' I rested my cheek against his soft belly and smelled his Dad-like smell, which is a mix of mouthwash, the leather from his belt (which holds his sword), and whatever detergent the hotel uses.

'Yes,' Dad said. 'Well, I'm very sorry it took so long. It was your mother's idea, you know, for you not to know the truth, and for us not to have any personal contact. She was worried about you growing up in the celebrity spotlight.'

'I know,' I said, still hugging him. 'I already met the reporters downstairs.'

'I'm very sorry about all that—'

I could hear his stomach juices digesting whatever he'd had for lunch. It was a comforting sound, but I felt bad for him anyway. All these years later, he is still clearly devastated over the loss of my beautiful, beautiful mother.

Well, who wouldn't be? She was an amazing lady.

I hoped the sight of me wouldn't be too painful for him.

'That's another reason your mother thought it would be safer for you not to know,' Dad went on. 'The press can be so intrusive. You have the right to grow up without being harassed. And from what I understand, even before they found out, you were already being picked on at school—'

I let go of him at last.

'Yes,' I said, looking up into his face. 'But didn't Princess Mia's mom want the same thing for her? And she's turned out all right. I think I will too.'

He laid his hands on both my shoulders and said, with a sigh, 'Yes, Olivia, I agree with you. You seem like a very special girl. But it wasn't easy for Mia, and it's not going to be easy for you, either.'

'I know,' I said. 'But I'm tougher than I look. And

I've already learned how to smile and wave. Look.'

I showed him the smile and wave that Princess Mia had taught me, though the effect was somewhat ruined by Snowball choosing that moment to jump up on me, because she's still a puppy, and she hasn't been properly trained.

'No, Snowball,' I said, taking hold of her front paws and giving them a gentle squeeze. 'Down.' I put her front paws back on the floor so she'd know 'down' meant keeping her paws on the floor. This is how you train puppies. I saw it once on a TV show.

'I guess it's been hard for you,' Dad said thoughtfully, 'living with the O'Tooles, and not having a . . . pet of your own.' It wasn't a question.

'Aw,' I said. I didn't want him to feel bad by letting him know how much things have stunk lately, especially with Annabelle and all, so I scooped Snowball up in my arms and buried my face in her soft, fluffy fur to hide my expression. 'It's been OK. And at least now I have . . . Snowball.'

'I'm glad you like her,' Dad said. 'Because in the future, you might be visiting her a lot more often. You see, I was wondering if you'd like to come live with us.'

Wednesday 6 May
9.45 p.m.
The Plaza Hotel

To say that I was shocked by this question would be the understatement of the universe. I was so astonished by it that I sort of dropped Snowball (well, not dropped her, really, but let her slither out of my arms, so that she ended up in a soft pile on the marble floor, looking confused).

I had to sit down before I ended up down there on the marble with her.

I guess Dad must have noticed my shock, since he took me by the arm and pulled me over to the brown leather couch. He made me sit down, then sat down beside me.

The couch was super soft and amazingly comfortable. Snowball clearly thought so too, since she scrambled up to sit on a pillow beside us.

'You won't hurt my feelings at all if you say no,' Dad said quickly. 'Please don't worry about that. I can totally understand if you'd rather stay with your aunt Catherine. After all, that's where you've lived all your life.'

I didn't say anything in reply to this. That's because I wasn't sure I could actually talk, I was still so surprised.

Also happy.

'Of course I've been wanting you to come live with me for a long time,' Dad went on. 'But, as your aunt has often pointed out, that would have violated your mother's wishes. A child needs stability, and also a mother, and I've never really been in a position in the past to offer you either of those things. But I think your aunt and even your mother would agree that things have changed quite a bit recently. They'll be changing even more soon—'

I looked up at him hopefully. 'They will? How?'

'Well, for one, I understand that your aunt and uncle are planning to move you to Qalif. That is unacceptable and something I simply won't allow. For another, whether we like it or not, the secret of your being a princess of Genovia is out. There's nothing we can do about that now. And, finally, your sister, Mia, is getting married, and—'

'She is?' I didn't mean to interrupt, but this was very startling news.

'Yes, she is. And she and her husband will be residing in Genovia, so your aunt's long-standing objection that there won't be stable female influence in the home is moot.'

I just stared at him. I couldn't believe any of this was happening. It was like a beautiful dream.

'You want me to come live with you in Genovia?' I asked.

'Yes,' he said. 'Do you know where that is?'

I nodded. I'd looked it up on Princess Mia's friend's phone. 'It's in between France and Italy.'

'Well, more or less,' he said. 'It's very small, but

has the loveliest median year-round temperature of any country in Europe, being situated as it is so idyllically on the Riviera—'

Before I could ask another question, the door to the library swung open, and Grandma came in, followed by a waiter holding a huge silver tray.

'I can't imagine when that child last had something to eat,' she said. 'So I had room service whip up a little snack. If I know Amelia, I'm sure all she fed you, Olivia, is junk food from the mini-bar of the limousine.'

I didn't see what was wrong with that, but I was still very excited when the waiter put the silver tray down on the large antique coffee table in front of our couch. My eyes bulged as I took in the 'little snack' room service had whipped up, which included:

- Bowls containing freshly cut strawberries, sugar cookies, chocolate truffles, and nuts
- A plate of multicoloured mini-cakes
- Plates with three different kinds of cheeses,

including the oozy creamy kind

- A plate of different kinds of sandwich meat – ham, salami, roast beef and turkey, along with some smoked salmon
- Tiny silver cups of mustard, mayonnaise, horseradish and cream cheese with matching tiny silver serving spoons
- A basket loaded with slices of white, whole wheat, rye, pumpernickel and French bread, along with assorted bagels

Coming from a wheat-free house, the sight of so much gluten almost made me cry for joy.

'Your Royal Highness,' the waiter said, handing me an elegant crystal goblet brimming with frothy brown liquid. 'Chocolate milk.'

There was a straw in it. The bendy kind!

'Thanks,' I squeaked. I don't think I could have gotten anything else out, even if I could have figured out what to say.

'Thank you, George,' Grandma said. 'That will be all.'

The waiter bowed and went away.

'Well,' Grandma said, sitting with elegant grace on the couch beside Dad, and helping herself to a small plate, on which she began to heap slices of ham. 'Did you ask her, Phillipe?'

'Yes,' Dad said. 'I did.'

'And?' Grandma put her plate of ham on to the floor for the dogs to eat. 'What did she say?'

'She hasn't had a chance to say anything yet, Mother. I think she's in shock. Where's Mia?'

'Where do you think? On the phone with that boyfriend of hers.'

'He's her fiancé now, Mother.'

I took a sip of the chocolate milk. It was ice-cold. When I'd swallowed, I said, 'I think I *am* in shock. This is the best chocolate milk I've ever tasted.'

'Really?' Grandma looked very interested. She was preparing another plate, this one of roast beef. 'Is it the drink, or your father? Don't you know he always wanted you to live with him? Your mother simply wouldn't allow it. Because of me, of course.'

'Mother,' Dad said in a warning tone.

'What?' Grandma asked with a shrug. 'It's true. I'm a terrible influence. Amelia's mother feels the same way. But Olivia is old enough now that I doubt she'll be morally corrupted by my scandalous ways—'

'Mother!' Dad looked stern now. He reached out and took away the plate of roast beef his mother was feeding to her new puppy.

'You see?' Grandma said to me as Snowball swallowed the roast beef that was already in her mouth. 'I'm incorrigible.'

'Well,' I said. 'You sort of are. You shouldn't feed dogs human food, especially from the table. Everyone knows that. It's probably what's making Rommel's fur fall out.'

Grandma's eyes widened. They were blue, like my dad's. 'Really? I don't think so. You know, I was walking a dog much like Rommel the day I met your grandfather. I was strolling down the Champs-Élysées wearing a cunning little cocktail dress I'd been saving for just such an occasion, pink – silk, of course – with shoes I'd had dyed to match, and this *adorable* little hat I got in—'

'Mother,' Dad said more sternly than ever.

She broke out of her reverie. 'Well,' she said. 'The girl *asked*. I was only—'

'She didn't ask, actually. The thing is, Olivia,' Dad said, handing me a plate on which he'd set a plain bagel loaded with cream cheese and smoked salmon, a fat, juicy strawberry and a sugar cookie, 'we haven't exactly discussed any of this yet with your aunt Catherine. In fact, she doesn't know you're here, only that you're with Mia—'

Whoa! So I knew something Aunt Catherine didn't know!

Of course, it wouldn't be long before Aunt Catherine knew. All she'd have to do was look on the news – or the Internet. I'm sure once those reporters downstairs uploaded their photos of me, Aunt Catherine – and Uncle Rick and Sara and Justin – were going to be in for a shock.

'We didn't figure there was much point in telling her,' Dad went on, 'unless we knew you'd actually be interested—'

'Genovia is the best place to live in the world,' Grandma interrupted, popping a petit four in her mouth. 'For one thing, the yachting is divine. And, of course, the food is to die for. You haven't lived until you've had the choux a la crème at Alberto's—'

'It would be a really big change,' Dad went on, ignoring his mother. 'It would mean coming to live in a palace, instead of a house—'

'But it's so much better to live in a palace,' Grandma pointed out. 'You can give your trash to a servant instead of having to drag it yourself all the way to the end of a driveway.'

Dad stared at Grandma. 'When have you ever had to take out your own trash, Mother?'

'And, of course, if you live with us, you'll have your own pony, Olivia,' Grandma went on. 'I had the loveliest pony when I was your age. I called him Zip. He ate apples straight out of my hand. I'm deathly allergic to horse hair, of course, and wept buckets of tears every time he was near, but it was worth it. I loved him so.'

'You'd have to switch schools,' Dad said, speaking as if Grandma hadn't said anything. 'But—'

'But the Royal Genovian Academy is right down the street from the palace,' Grandma interrupted. 'It's a truly excellent school, with its own stables where you can learn to ride, and very rigorous entrance standards. They don't let in just *anyone*, like the public schools in America are forced to.'

'I don't know if I could get into a school with rigorous entrance standards,' I said awkwardly, because I didn't want them to be disappointed in me. 'I mean, Aunt Catherine had me tested, and my intelligence is only average.'

Dad and Grandma exchanged glances.

'Did your aunt tell you that, Olivia?' Dad asked. 'That you were average?'

'No,' I said. 'My step-cousin Sara did. She overheard my aunt and her dad talking. But I know it's true. Because I'm not in any advanced placement classes. I mean, I get good enough grades, I guess. But I really have to study. The truth is, I'm . . . well, I'm completely average. There's nothing special about me. Nothing at all.'

I felt nervous admitting it, but I had to tell them, since they'd have found out eventually anyway.

'Except for drawing . . .' I added, remembering at the last minute. 'I'm a very good drawer according to my teacher, Ms Dakota, except that I need to work on my perspective. I was even admitted to an art school, with a scholarship. But Aunt Catherine said I was too young.'

Grandma brightened. 'You obviously inherited that from me. I was always exquisite at drawing, myself. And, you know, the Royal Genovian Academy has an excellent art programme. I shouldn't brag, but the great Picasso saw me drawing one day on the Rue de Rivoli in Paris – I remember I was wearing a pair of chinos that I got hand-tailored at a lovely little shop in Capri; I'll have to take you there when you're older, you haven't the figure for them now, of course – and the great master himself offered to–'

Dad cut her off. 'No, he didn't, Mother.' To me, he said, 'I don't think you're average, Olivia. I don't think there's anything average about you.'

'I've only just met you,' Grandma said, 'and I don't think you're a bit average. No average person could make Rommel do *that*.' She pointed at the hairless poodle, who was curled up against my hip, sleeping soundly with my thigh as a pillow for his head. 'Rommel hates everyone.'

'Including me,' Dad said.

'Including Phillipe,' Grandma agreed.

'Mia thinks you're special too, Olivia,' Dad went on. 'The fact is we all think you're special, and we'd be very honoured to have you come live with us, at least for part of the year. But we'd understand if you'd rather stay with your aunt.'

'Speak for yourself,' Grandma said, taking a sip of whatever it was she was drinking. 'I'd never understand it. I think it would be an utter waste, and quite frankly a disaster.'

'Your grandmother has a tendency to exaggerate,' Dad said, 'as you'll find out the more you get to know her.'

'I suppose we could come to New Jersey to visit you,' Grandma said. She didn't sound very enthusiastic about this last part. She said the words 'New Jersey' like they were a disease she hoped not to catch. 'But not Qalif. Rommel doesn't take well to hot weather.'

'Rommel doesn't take well to *any* weather,' Dad said, in a bitter voice.

To me he said, 'Why don't you take some time to think it over? Want some more chocolate milk?'

I shook my head. I was still in so much shock I didn't know what to think.

So, instead of thinking, I picked up the bagel Dad had made for me and sank my teeth into it. It had been so long since I'd last had bread I'd almost forgotten how good it tasted.

Then I remembered something, and after

swallowing what was in my mouth, said, 'Dad?'

He had just taken a big bite of his bagel. 'Hmm?' he said.

'How did you know I like cream cheese and smoked salmon on my bagels?' I asked.

'Oh, that's easy,' Grandma said, while Dad struggled to chew before answering. 'It's his favourite too.'

I guess there's more you can inherit from your family than just eye colour and a talent for drawing. You can also inherit thrones, and a liking for smoked salmon.

Wednesday 6 May
11 p.m.
The Plaza Hotel

It's way past my bedtime (which is nine thirty in Cranbrook), but I can't sleep. I'm too excited!

Plus, I'm sleeping in a strange place . . . the spare guest room in my grandmother's penthouse suite in New York City!

I've never slept in such a huge bed, under such an elegant canopy, between such comfortable sheets, in such nice pyjamas (which my grandmother loaned to me. They're made out of silk and have the letter 'G' on them . . . for Genovia. They're princess pyjamas! Nishi would die of excitement).

But none of these things is why I've made the decision I have:

I'm moving to Genovia.

Don't get me wrong: it's definitely lovely to sleep in silk pyjamas and a canopy bed (with an adorable fluffy white poodle puppy next to me).

It's great to think that I'm not only going to have my own pony some day, but also a chance to get to go to art school, and not even on a scholarship.

But to get a father, a grandmother and a sister who *actually care about me* on top of all that?

Sorry. No contest.

I don't want to make Aunt Catherine feel bad by moving in with Dad and Grandma and Mia (who turns out to be a hugger. She hugged me so hard before she left to go back to her own apartment tonight I thought she was going to break my ribs. In a good way!).

But I'm pretty sure Aunt Catherine will understand. She has her design business to worry about, and Uncle Rick and Sara and Justin, and the exciting new opportunities waiting for them all in

Qalif. She'll probably be relieved when she finds out
I'm not going with them!

I'm definitely going to miss Nishi, though. But
Dad said I could have her come visit whenever
I wanted!

I can't imagine how hard it's going to be, starting over at a whole new middle school where I don't know anyone, in a brand-new country, where they speak a whole different language (that I also happen to be a princess of).

But at least in Genovia there won't be the one thing from New Jersey I'll DEFINITELY never miss: Annabelle Jenkins.

This has truly been the greatest day of my life.

Maybe *that's* why I can't sleep! I never want it to end.

Thursday 7 May
11.24 a.m.
Bergdorf Goodman

Normally at this time I'd be in French class at Cranford Middle School.

But instead I'm in a fancy department store getting fitted for a whole new wardrobe because Grandma says the eyes of the entire world are on me right now and it's my time to 'shine' (this isn't at all scary).

(Yes, it is a little scary. We had to sneak out of the delivery doors of the hotel through the kitchen just to avoid the paparazzi, who are *still* waiting out front! It's insane.)

I've already learned more things about being a princess in just a few hours than I've learned the whole five years I've been taking French class.

Like that when you're a princess, you can't say 'What?' when you don't understand something.

You're supposed to say, 'I beg your pardon?' or 'Excuse me?'

Also that it's rude when you're a princess to put ketchup on things before you've even tasted them. It's an insult to the chef's cooking. You have to taste it first, *then* decide if it is not 'seasoned enough' to your particular liking.

Only then may you ask for the ketchup, which it turns out room service has to bring all the way from downstairs, so it takes a really long time if you live in the penthouse.

I don't know how I'm ever going to remember all this stuff, which is why it's good I have this notebook to write it all down in, especially considering that this morning when I woke up, I didn't even know where I was!

Then I looked down and saw Snowball curled up

beside my head and Rommel stretched out by my feet and the sun shining through the fancy windows leading to a balcony looking out over Central Park – Central Park in *New York City*! – and I remembered everything that had happened yesterday and I was like:

'I'm at my dad's! With my grandma! And this is her dog, and this is her other dog that has no hair, and they want me to come live with them in Genovia, the country of which I am also a *princess*!'

And then I nearly fell over dead of a heart attack. But fortunately I was still in bed, so I didn't have very far to fall.

I could smell toast (real toast!), so I hurried up and brushed my teeth and got dressed and went out into the dining room, and there was Grandma reading the paper in her robe in front of a table with more food piled on to it than I'd ever seen, including:

- Piles and piles of warm golden waffles
- Gobs of fluffy whipped cream

- Bowls of glistening red strawberries
- Silver pitchers of real maple syrup
- Crystal goblets of orange juice
- Eggs and soldiers (which are soft-boiled eggs and strips of toast)

I'd never had this last thing before, but it turns out what you do is you crack open the top of the shell of the soft-boiled egg, then dip a strip of the buttery toast into the warm, gooey egg yolk. It's the most delicious thing in the whole world (well, aside from the waffles).

And in the end it turned out not to even need ketchup.

Anyway, as I was eating the biggest, best breakfast I had ever had, with Snowball at my side, Grandma put down the paper and said, 'Your father has a conference call with the Genovian parliament, and your sister has a personal appointment. So I am taking you shopping.'

'Shopping? What about school?'

'School? Why are you worrying about school?

You haven't decided you want to stay in *New Jersey*, have you?'

'Grandma,' I said. 'New Jersey is my home state. I was born there. You have to stop saying it that way.'

'What way?'

'Like it's a dirty word.'

She shrugged and passed a bit of bacon to Rommel, who was crouched beside her chair. 'Fine. If you love *New Jersey* so much that you want to live there for the rest of your life and never travel the world or have new experiences, far be it from me to stop you.'

'I didn't say that. I've decided I want to live in Genovia with you and Dad and Princess Mia. But—'

Grandma almost smiled, but not all the way. Her mouth doesn't really move all that much. Princess Mia told me this is because she's 'had a lot of work done'.

'Well, if that's the case, why are you worrying about your old school? You'll be attending the Royal Genovian Academy from now on. But as we haven't enrolled you yet they can hardly count you as absent.'

'Yes, but I'm still enrolled at my old school, and if I don't show up there today they'll mark it as an unexcused absence and I'll get a demerit.'

'A demerit?' she asked in astonishment. 'Merely for enjoying a day of shopping with your grandmother?'

'Shopping isn't an excusable absence. An excusable absence is like when my friend Nishi's grandmother got sick with appendicitis and had to go to the hospital. Nishi was allowed to skip school to visit her, because that was an emergency.

Shopping isn't an emergency.'

'It most certainly is,' Grandma said, looking offended. 'We can't allow you to go about in *that* any more.' She pointed at my school uniform. 'The paparazzi will undoubtedly photograph you again today and then think we are cruelly mistreating you by providing you with only one outfit. How is that not an emergency?'

That's when she showed me the front page of the paper she was reading.

'That's ME!' I cried, dropping my toast (it was OK, though, because Rommel and Snowball snatched it up, even though it landed butter-side down on the floor).

'Yes,' she said. 'It is. So is this.' She

lifted up another newspaper from the pile beside her and showed me its front page as well.

SIXTH-GRADE SENSATION!
PINT-SIZED PRINCESS FROM NEW JERSEY SECOND IN LINE TO GENOVIAN THRONE

Fortunately, this time I wasn't holding any food I could drop.

'Wow!' was all I could think of to say. I couldn't help wondering if Annabelle Jenkins had seen the paper. If so, I bet she was pretty upset about it. It had to be killing her that *I* was the one being called a sixth-grade sensation, and not her.

Not all the papers had such flattering headlines about me, though (I hoped Annabelle didn't see *those*). Some of the reporters were still writing mean things, like that my dad had purposefully kept me 'hidden away in Cranbrook' all these years so his mom, the Genovian people and the press wouldn't find out about me, because I was his 'shameful secret'.

This was so not what had happened! Well, it was – I'd definitely been hidden away in Cranbrook, but not because I was anyone's 'shameful secret.'

Grandma must have noticed me getting upset, since she said, 'Part of the job of being a royal is receiving a great deal of attention from the press. Your face on the cover of any newspaper or magazine will help it to sell. But you can't expect everything written about you to be positive.'

'But some of it isn't even *true*!'

Grandma looked amused. 'My dear, being half American yourself, you must know that the American people's right to express their opinions is guaranteed by something called the First Amendment. Until those opinions are found to be proven factually incorrect, they can go on expressing them as long as they like.'

I did know this, but it still didn't seem fair. 'Well, can we please prove their opinions factually incorrect?'

'Of course. In due time, we shall issue a statement. In the meantime, we need to take you shopping.

When you look your best, you feel your best, and no one could possibly feel their best in *that*.' She pointed at my skirt.

'Fine, Grandma,' I said with a sigh. 'But, like I said, I'm pretty sure Dr Bushy won't allow clothes shopping as an excused absence.'

'And what, pray tell, is a bushy?'

'He's not a what, Grandma, he's a who. He's the principal of my school. I'd like to prove my haters factually incorrect by leaving Cranbrook without any demerits, if that's OK with you.'

'It's Grandmère, not Grandma, and don't be ridiculous. Princesses can't get demerits. But I will telephone this "Bushy" person if you're so worried, and explain the situation.'

Grandma, I mean Grandmère, calling the CMS administrative office was probably one of the weirdest things I'd ever witnessed, and I'd witnessed a lot of weird things in the past twenty-four hours.

'Hello, is this Cranbrook Middle School?' Grandmère asked after I dialled for her (because she isn't very good at using phones, even regular ones).

'Oh yes, quite, very well, how do you do? This is the Dowager Princess Clarisse Renaldo of Genovia phoning on behalf of my granddaughter Princess Olivia Grace Clarisse Mignonette Harrison. I would like to speak to Dr Bushy. I beg your pardon? He's in a meeting? Well, please inform him that my granddaughter will not be able to attend school today, as she is in dire need of a new wardrobe. Thank you.'

I'm pretty sure Mrs Singh, the school administrative aide, probably thought that was a crank call, but Grandmère hung up before she could ask.

Then Grandmère went to 'put on her face' (which is what she calls putting on her make-up) and get dressed.

Now we're here in this store, 'assembling my wardrobe' with the help of Grandmère's 'personal stylist', which is really just a fancy name for a lady who works in the store but is only in charge of one customer: my grandma, and now me.

Grandmère's personal stylist, Brigitte, is super nice, especially since she allows dogs in her store

(Grandmère let me bring Snowball since she brought Rommel), but I don't know how anyone would think trying on clothes for *over four hours* is fun. Maybe someone interested in fashion like Annabelle Jenkins or Sara would, but not me.

Although Grandmère says that fashion is important because it immediately communicates to others your sense of style (which I have not yet had a chance to cultivate, having been forced to wear a uniform to school for most of my life) and even helps boost your self-esteem.

But my self-esteem is not feeling so boosted right now since in the last two hours Brigitte has made me try on (and then Grandmère has bought):

- Ten pairs of trousers (all kinds, from jeans to what Brigitte calls 'casual slacks')
- Eleven skirts ('flared to fitted')
- Thirty dresses (according to my grandma, 'Princesses need quite a lot of dresses as they are always being called upon to attend formal occasions, be they polo matches, balls, or

benefits to raise awareness of the shrinking ice shelves')

- More shoes than I can count, from boots to loafers to dancing shoes to what Grandmère calls 'trainers' (which I later found out are sneakers. I don't know what she thinks I'm training for, other than being a princess)

- Underwear (twenty pairs, which fortunately Brigitte did NOT make me try on, though Grandmère did go on for quite a long time about the importance of 'breathability' and 'all-cotton' until I wanted to die)

- Some things Grandmère called 'foundation garments,' but which I finally realized were bras! My new grandma made me try on bras! Right in front of her! Like I even have anything to put in them! Fortunately Brigitte realized this, and so really they were only what Nishi calls 'sports bras', and Brigitte called 'training bras'. Still, I wanted to die again

- Socks (twenty pairs)
- Layering Tees (ten)
- Sweaters (ten – it is always warm in Genovia, Grandmère said, but apparently I am going to learn to ski)
- Long-sleeve blouses and shirts (twenty. And Grandmère wouldn't even let me get shirts that said anything on them, such as WHO FARTED? in sparkles, which I thought would be hilarious, but she did not)
- What Grandmère called 'outerwear' – coats and jackets
- And finally 'accessories' – hats, gloves and bags, but no jewellery because, as Grandmère said, 'You're going to have access to the finest collection of crown jewels in all of Europe.'

Really, it was all just too much, and after a while I wanted to yell, 'STOP!' I hardly have any clothes outside my school uniform anyway, and I kind of like it that way, because sometimes having too many choices is confusing.

So I said I needed to take a break and Brigitte looked at me with kind of a concerned expression and asked if I wanted some water and I said yes, and she brought me a glass on a silver tray and now I'm drinking it in here alone and writing this.

Having a family of your own and being a princess is fun and all, but parts of it are very exhausting and confusing and even a little embarrassing.

Thursday 7 May
3.45 p.m.
Limousine

< NishiGirl   OlivGrace >

Hey, it's me. I finally got my own phone!

No way!!!! I'm so excited for u!!! Where r u? Y weren't u in school 2day? Everyone was talking about u!!!

LOL! I went shopping with my grandmother.

THAT IS NOT AN EXCUSABLE ABSENCE!!!!!

I know. I was afraid I was going to get a demerit!

< NishiGirl   OlivGrace >

They can't give u a demerit. U r a princess!!!

That's what my grandma said!

LOLOLOLOL! We saw u on the news last night! U r EVERYWHERE!

Ugh, I know. They're saying terrible things. None of them is true.

LOL I know that! It was ur mom who didn't want people to know.

How did u know that???

Because Annabelle said so yesterday. Remember?

Oh right. I forgot. A lot has happened since yesterday.

Also because ur sister just said it on TV.

She did??? WHEN???

Just now. How could u not know?
U royals need to communicate more.

Really?!? I'm with her in the limo right now!

Really? It must have been
pre-taped. What r u doing?

My grandma just tried to take me to a fancy beauty
salon for a makeover! But Princess Mia found out
and showed up and stopped her before they could
do anything more than give me spiral curls.

WHY????

She said I don't need one. She
says I'm beautiful just the way I am.

Awww!!! It's true.

Thank u. U r beautiful just the way u r too.

< NishiGirl   OlivGrace >

Thanks, I know. But I'd like a makeover anyway. I want to get my nose pierced and my hair dyed purple.

U would look SO GOOD with a pierced nose and purple hair. But ur grandmother would kill you.

I bet urs would too, especially considering she's a princess and so are u. But u'd just have to explain that princesses can have pierced noses and purple hair and still be regal.

True. So what are people saying at school?

Mostly how cool it is that u r a princess. Except Sara. She says u r ungrateful.

Ungrateful? For what???

For everything her dad has done for u.

What??? What has her dad ever done for me???

< NishiGirl   OlivGrace >

I know! I was like, 'U mean not getting her a phone or computer when both u and Justin have one? Or not taking her for rides in one of his stolen Ferraris?'

No, u didn't!!!

Yes, I did!

What did Sara say???

She didn't say anything. She got so mad she got up and went to go sit at Annabelle's table.

NOOOOOO!

Yes! And Annabelle LET HER SIT THERE!

Great. So now there's an official 'I Hate Olivia' lunch table at school.

Oh, what do u care? U r the princess of Genovia!

< NishiGirl   OlivGrace >

I know. Guess what? My sister is getting married and asked me to be a junior bridesmaid in her royal wedding this summer!

☺☺☺☺☺☺☺☺☺!!!!!

And guess what else: u r invited too.

♡☺☺☺♡☺☺♡☺☺☺♡!!!!!!!

And guess what else: my dad asked me to come live with him in Genovia!!!

X_X. ← That's me. I'm dead now.
U just killed me with happiness for u.

Nooooo! Don't die! I need u to help me! U r the princess expert!

It's true, I am. And it's great to be able to txt u about it now, but I'm still going to miss u!!!!

< NishiGirl   OlivGrace >

I'm going to miss u too! But my dad says u can come visit any time! Ur family too! He'll send the royal jet for u so it will be free!

♡☺♡☺♡☺♡☺♡☺♡☺♡!!!!!!!!!!!

So I guess that means u'll come?

Of course!!! I've always wanted to see the inside of a palace. A real one, not the Beauty and the Beast one at Disney World.

Well, now u r going to get to.
We're BOTH going to get to!

This is so GREAT! I'm going to ask my mom, but I'm sure she'll say yes because Genovia has no human rights violations and doesn't treat women like second-class citizens (unlike Qalif)!

Well, that's a relief! Oops, I gotta go, we're back at the hotel! Text u later!

Text u later, UR ROYAL HIGHNESS!!!

Thursday 7 May
8.45 p.m.
My Old Room,
Cranbrook, New Jersey

I am sitting in my old room crying as I write this. So if you see any blobby marks on the page, that's what they are. Also, Snowball keeps trying to lick up my tears, so if you see wrinkle marks, they're from her paws.

But mostly they're tears.

I'm crying because when we got back to the hotel, something horrible happened.

It's not my dad's fault. He did the best he could.

But sometimes, even if you're a princess, things don't go your way. Sometimes all the brainpower,

nice clothes and royal bodyguards in the world can't
save you.

When I walked into the living room with
Grandmère and Mia, I was totally surprised to see
Aunt Catherine and Uncle Rick sitting there with
my dad.

In some distant part of my brain, I thought
maybe they'd come to tell me how glad they were

for me finally reuniting with my dad, and me turning out to be a princess.

Until I saw Annabelle's dad, Mr Jenkins, sitting there with them. Then I knew that probably wasn't why they were there.

It turned out I was right.

Uncle Rick stood up and said in a very mean voice, 'Finally. There she is. Olivia, get your things. You're going home right now.'

No 'Hi, Olivia, how are you?' or 'Gee, Olivia, it's great to see you.' Just 'Get your things, you're going home right now.'

'Um,' I said. 'I know I missed school today, but it was an excused absence. Grandmère totally phoned in—'

'I don't care,' Uncle Rick said. 'Go and get your things.'

'Rick,' Aunt Catherine said. She looked like she'd been crying. 'Must you—?'

That's when my step-uncle told her to shut up, and that it was all her fault for being 'stupid enough' to have let me leave Cranbrook with

Princess Mia in the first place.

Then my dad stood up and said something *very* mean to Uncle Rick for telling my aunt to shut up, and Princess Mia took my hand and said, 'Let's go into the other room,' and we both stepped out on to the balcony and she started pointing out landmarks in Central Park in a way that I could tell meant she did not want me to overhear what was happening in the other room.

'Did I get you in trouble?' I asked her nervously.

'You?' She looked surprised. 'Of course not! It's just grown-up stuff. Don't worry about it.'

I hate it when adults say this, like I'm not old enough to understand. Because, obviously, this involved me, and I had a right to know what was going on.

'But why is Uncle Rick so mad?' I asked. 'And why is Mr Jenkins here? I thought Aunt Catherine wrote you that permission slip saying it was all right for me to come with you to New York.'

'She did,' she said with a sigh. 'But things have got a bit more complicated—'

And then she told me something that made me want to throw up everything we'd had for lunch (at a restaurant that my grandmother said was her favourite, the Four Seasons, but they didn't serve food from the four seasons, such as watermelon, pumpkin pie, beef stew and chocolate Easter bunnies, which was disappointing).

It turns out Nishi had been right all along. Only it wasn't just the two Ferraris.

All the trips to New York City that I never got to go on. The phones and laptops and flat-screen TVs for everyone's room but mine. Not to mention all that fancy carpeting that would only have been ruined by the pet I'd always wanted and was forbidden to have.

All of it. They'd stolen all of it. From me.

'Nothing's been proven yet,' Princess Mia went on carefully. 'The Royal Genovian Guard is still investigating. It was only when you mentioned in one of your letters to Dad that you were moving to Qalif that anyone even became suspicious. But we believe your aunt and uncle have been using money meant for you to fund their business, which simply isn't right—'

In that moment something shifted and I felt as if I finally understood what Ms Dakota had been saying about perspective. The new information acted like a vanishing point and suddenly everything I knew about Aunt Catherine and Uncle Rick lined up and I could see the truth about them. It wasn't a very nice truth. It was one I'd been trying hard not to let myself see.

'That's why they want me back, isn't it?' I asked, looking up at Princess Mia. 'They don't want to give up the money Dad sends for me every month.'

'No,' she said quickly. 'I'm sure that's not true. Your aunt loves you very much—'

I shook my head. Aunt Catherine, love me? She may have tried to make it look that way on the outside – she fed me and gave me clothes and let me live in a house that was pretty to look at.

But, if she loved me, why had she never once hugged me? I'd already been hugged more in one day living with my dad and Princess Mia than I had in all the years I'd lived with Aunt Catherine. Not to mention eaten more gluten.

But I didn't bring this up. Instead, I asked, 'So then why did they bring Mr Jenkins with them?'

'They hired Mr Jenkins a few days ago when we began questioning their right to take you to Qalif,' she said.

That explained a lot . . . like how Annabelle had overheard her dad talking about my being a princess.

'Your aunt still has legal guardianship of you, however,' Mia said, looking worriedly at the French doors, 'so if she's changed her mind and refuses to allow you to stay with us any longer, there's nothing we can do . . . at least for now. But I promise that Dad will never rest until he gets permanent custody of you. It just might—'

I don't know where it came from, but suddenly this voice I'd never heard before burst out of me. It said, 'Noooooo!'

I ran back inside from the terrace and threw my arms round my father's waist and yelled, 'I won't! I won't go back with them to New Jersey!'

Dad hugged me and patted me on my newly styled head and leaned down to whisper, 'Be brave, Olivia. It may take a while, but we'll figure this whole thing out, and make it right.'

Be brave? They're always expecting princesses to be brave, and in books and movies it always turns out all right, but that's because there's usually ray guns or magic involved.

There isn't any magic in real life, or ray guns, either. And, no matter how much brainpower you have, it doesn't work against the law, like when someone – such as my aunt Catherine – is your legal guardian.

And how long is a while? No one ever tells you.

The only good part is that when I went to hug Grandmère goodbye, she said, 'Don't forget this,' and handed me Snowball on a leash.

I had already been crying, but I REALLY started crying when that happened.

'But, Grandmère,' I said, 'she's *your* dog, not mine!'

'Don't be ridiculous,' Grandmère said. 'She's

yours now. She positively adores
you. She'd be miserable without
you.'

Uncle Rick tried to say something
about his allergies, but Grandmère
gave him a look that caused him to shut his mouth
and not say another word until we were in the car
driving back to Cranbrook, and even then it was
only to complain about the fact that he thought we
were being followed.

I turned round and looked, but I couldn't see
what he was talking about, and Aunt Catherine told
him to stop being so silly, that we'd left the hotel
through the delivery door in order to avoid the
reporters out front and walked four blocks to the
car since Uncle Rick wouldn't pay for valet parking,
and I'd worn one of Dad's old ski caps as a disguise
so no one could possibly have recognized me and
that she had a headache.

So now I am back in my old room in my old
house and it is like it was all a dream. The only
proof I have that any of it ever happened is that I

can flip through the pages of this notebook and see what I wrote (and drew), and of course Snowball, who is asleep on my lap.

Well, there's also Sara, who keeps stopping by my room to show me paparazzi photos of me on her phone (Uncle Rick took my phone away. He says it isn't 'safe' for me to have it because I am too inexperienced and it might get hacked, so he is keeping it for now).

All Justin wants to know is what it was like to ride in a limo.

'Good,' I said. 'I got to drink all the soda I wanted.'

'Soda is fattening,' Justin said.

'You would know,' I said.

'Are you calling me fat?' he asked.

'Your head is.'

'You think you're so great,' he said, 'just because you're a princess.'

'No,' I said. 'I think I'm so great because I am.'

'You better watch it,' he said. 'Or tomorrow you're gonna get it.'

'You better watch it,' I said. 'Or some day I'm

going to put you in my dungeon and never let you out and all they're going to find are bones.'

He didn't look very scared. He saw Snowball lick some of my tears and said, 'Dogs have more germs in their mouths than in their buttholes,' and walked away.

I know it is wrong to hate people, but I hate Justin.

I don't hate Sara, though, because she complimented my new hair, which Princess Mia had allowed Paolo – Grandmère's beautician – to style into spiral curls:

'It's basically just like your old hair, only more organized.'

Maybe when I wake up tomorrow morning, this will have been a nightmare, and I'll be back in the guest room at the Plaza.

Probably not, though.

Friday 8 May
9.00 a.m.
Biology Class

It wasn't a nightmare. I'm still in Cranbrook.

It's so weird being here. Everyone is staring at me.

I guess I can't blame them, considering what happened when I walked up to my locker this morning.

Of course the last person I wanted to see – Annabelle Jenkins – was waiting there for me, her eyes crackling with meanness.

I thought about turning round and walking right back out of school, but unfortunately Nishi was with me. She must have known what I was thinking, since she took my arm and said under her breath, 'Don't worry, it's going to be OK.'

Except it *wasn't* OK.

'Well, look who's slumming it back in Cranbrook,' Annabelle said. 'Her Royal Highness, Princess Olivia of Genovia herself.'

If everyone hadn't *already* been staring at me before Annabelle made that crack, they sure did then.

And it only got worse after that, of course.

'Look, Annabelle,' I said to her as I spun my combination. 'Can't we just try to get along?'

'Is that some of your dad's famous Genovian diplomacy?' she demanded acidly.

'No. It's an honest question.'

'An honest question,' she repeated with a laugh, putting on a performance for all her friends, who were standing around, watching. 'Aw, look at the pwetty pwincess, with the new pwetty pwincess hair.'

I remembered what Princess Mia had said to do when someone pays you a compliment, and said, in my most gracious voice, 'Why, thank you, Annabelle.'

She stopped laughing. 'I was kidding, you idiot. I think your hair looks terrible.'

Now she was just being ridiculous. My hair looked awesome, and even she had to know it.

'Come on, Annabelle,' Nishi said, trying to help. 'Why do you have to be that way?'

'Stay out of it, Fishy,' Annabelle said. 'This is between me and the princess.'

'Annabelle,' I said, 'I don't want to fight with you.'

'Too late,' Annabelle said. 'You and me, after school. And from what I hear, Big Sister Mia isn't going to be around this time to save you.'

'Really, Annabelle,' I said, a little wearily, because I had been through a lot in the past forty-eight hours. 'What did I ever do to you?'

'Oh, you know,' Annabelle said, her eyes narrowing. 'Don't act like you don't.'

'No,' I said. 'I really don't have any idea what you're talking about.'

'You *princess*,' Annabelle snarled. 'You think you're better than me!'

Then she pushed me – *hard* – into my locker.

For the second time in a week, I thought I was going to die . . .

. . . until a female Genovian bodyguard appeared from out of nowhere, slammed Annabelle up against the wall and said into her walkie-talkie, 'Situation in Hallway A. Situation with the princess in Hallway A.'

All I had time to think was, Where did *she* come from? before a *platoon* of Royal Genovian Guards showed up and hustled a weeping Annabelle – in handcuffs! off to Dr Bushy's office.

'But I didn't mean it!' Annabelle was crying. 'I didn't mean anything by it! Olivia and I are friends. Just ask her! Olivia and I are *best* friends! We were only playing around—'

The female bodyguard looked back at me, her long ponytail swinging. 'Are you two friends?'

I couldn't help feeling a little bad for Annabelle, since it seemed pretty clear that what Nishi had said about her was true: she was super insecure. I know from my wildlife illustration research that animals are only aggressive when they feel threatened (or are seeking prey to eat).

And Annabelle seemed pretty frightened at finding herself in handcuffs.

But at the same time, I'd been frightened at finding myself pushed into my locker!

I shook my head. 'No,' I said. 'We are not friends.'

The bodyguard nodded. 'That's what I thought,' she said, and nodded again to her fellow guards, who took a sobbing Annabelle away.

Nishi helped as I tried to find all the things that had spilled out of my notebook organizer when Annabelle had pushed me.

'Wow,' Nishi said. 'That was basically the coolest thing I've ever seen.'

'What happened just now?' I shook my head. 'No, that was not cool.'

'OK,' Nishi agreed. 'Maybe what Annabelle did wasn't cool, but you can't take it personally. I think it comes with the territory of being a princess. Or at least a princess in the same school as Annabelle. But those bodyguards? *They* were cool. Where did they come from? I thought you said your aunt and step-uncle weren't going to let you be a princess any more.'

'I know,' I said. 'But Uncle Rick also said last night he thought we were being followed home.'

'This is total royal spy stuff!' Nishi looked around happily. 'That's so cool! I wish I was a princess being spied on and protected by cool royal bodyguards!'

'Yeah.' I clutched my organizer to my chest. 'I

think it seems better when it's happening to other people than when it's happening to you.'

I also really hope the royal bodyguards are still around at three o'clock, which is when Annabelle said she's going to strike again.

Friday 8 May
2.25 p.m.
Social Studies Class

People were *fighting* to sit by me at lunch. Not exactly fist-fighting, but shoving one another.

Like having royal ninja bodyguards who appear from nowhere, this sounds better than it was. I just wanted to sit with my normal friends, like Nishi and Netta and Quetta and Beth Chandler.

But all these people who'd normally NEVER want to sit near us (such as Justin and his friends) kept elbowing for space at our table!

Then I found out Justin was SELLING TICKETS to sit near me!

Seven inches of space at my lunch table was going for as much as EIGHT DOLLARS!

It still seems unbelievable to me that my step-cousin, who once told me never even to speak to him at school, was selling tickets to sit near me.

Then again, he didn't give me so much as a penny! So I guess I shouldn't be surprised.

He is just like his father.

It's OK, though, because Dr Bushy noticed what was happening (since there were so many fights over seating at my table. Sabine – that's my personal bodyguard, the one with the ponytail – kept having to break them up).

If I were to rate the best moments of my life (so far), they would go (in order):

1. When I met my dad for the first time.

2. When my dad asked me to live with him in Genovia.

3. When the art school called and said they wanted to offer me that scholarship because I'd drawn Tippy the Turtle so well.

4. When Annabelle Jenkins was about to give me a beat-down and I looked up and saw Princess Mia standing by that limo.

5. When Dr Bushy stormed over today to grab Justin by the back of his neck and said, 'What is the meaning of this?' very loudly in front of everyone over by my lunch table and money started falling out of Justin's pockets and Beth Chandler got the whole thing on video and then said she's going to post it to her sister's YouTube channel.

So Justin got sent to Dr Bushy's office. It was *fantastic*.

That is the good news.

The bad news is that Annabelle Jenkins's father threatened to sue the school district for harassment, so Dr Bushy let her *out* of his office with only a demerit.

He also said that until 'this matter is settled', Sabine and all the rest of the Royal Genovian Guards would have to stay fifty feet away from Annabelle while she's on school property.

I guess Dr Bushy is still mad about that time Lars wouldn't let him take a selfie with me in the CMS car park.

Which means when three o'clock rolls round and I go out to the courtyard to catch my bus home, I am just going to have to be brave, like my father said, and hope that my fists are quicker than Annabelle's.

Friday 8 May
3.45 p.m.
My Room,
Cranbrook, New Jersey

They weren't.

I didn't even see her coming. When Annabelle's fist landed between my eyes, it knocked me down flat.

As I lay there blinking up at the sky, wondering what all the stars were doing out even though it was daytime, the next thing I saw after Annabelle's mean face was Sabine's. She was leaning over me saying, 'Princess? Princess Olivia? How many fingers am I holding up?'

'Two,' I said. My voice sounded strange.

Sabine nodded crisply enough to make her ponytail bounce and said, 'You'll live. I see we need to work on your self-defence skills.'

'Tell me about it.'

She smiled – the first time I'd ever seen her smile – then moved away as she said into her headset, 'The princess will be fine. Bring the cars round.'

Next my step-cousin Justin's face appeared.

'You can get up now,' he said. 'Annabelle's gone.'

Only I found that I felt much more comfortable on the ground. So I stayed were I was, watching the stars spin round and round.

'She's bleeding!' I heard a familiar voice cry. Ms Dakota, I thought. I wondered who she was talking about. Who was bleeding?

'One of the guards went to get a first aid kit.' That was Nishi. 'Olivia, can you get up? Come on, you guys, let's help her.'

Then Nishi and Beth Chandler and the twins pulled me up to my feet. After everything stopped spinning, I saw that tons of people were gathered around staring at me, including my art teacher, Ms Dakota. She pressed a wad of tissue paper that she'd pulled from her purse to my nose, which seemed to be running. A lot.

'Tilt your head forward, Olivia,' she said kindly, 'and pinch your nose.'

I tilted my head forward and pinched my nose. The stars had finally disappeared and the sky had gone back to an ordinary blue anyway.

'Man,' Justin said. 'That was a good strategy, just laying there like you were dead. Annabelle got so scared, she ran off. Your goons caught her halfway down the block. They probably have her in jail by now.'

'No thanks to you!' Nishi yelled at him. 'You were standing right there! Why didn't you try to stop her?'

'It wasn't my fight,' Justin said, looking genuinely surprised.

'Catherine's going to kill you,' Sara said, pointing at the front of my shirt. 'You got blood all over yourself.'

I looked down at the front of my shirt. It had been white. Now it was stained with drops of bright red.

'Don't listen to her,' Nishi ordered me, giving Sara a very dirty look. 'Keep pinching your nose, like Ms Dakota said.'

'Yes,' Ms Dakota said. 'Your nose is still bleeding a little, Olivia.'

So that's what the runny stuff was. Not snot, like I'd thought, but blood.

'What's happening out here?' I heard Dr Bushy's voice thunder as the doors to the school swung open. 'Why are you people just standing around? Why is no one getting on their buses?'

'Use your eyes, Paul,' Ms Dakota snapped. 'What do you *think* happened?'

I couldn't move my head to look because Ms Dakota was still holding her tissues to my nose, but I guessed by the change in his voice – it got considerably softer – that Dr Bushy noticed all the blood on my shirt.

'Oh, dear,' he said. 'Was it–?'

'Of course it was,' Ms Dakota said.

'Olivia,' Dr Bushy said. 'I mean, er, Your Royal Highness . . . may I just say . . . I'm, er, very sorry. I never thought she would go this far.'

I remembered everything Mia and my grandmother and Dad and even Nishi had taught me about being a princess. Princess are never ungracious and they don't hold grudges, either. They accept apologies when they're given sincerely.

So I nodded to Dr Bushy – as gracefully as I could while pinching my nose – and said, 'It's all right.'

I don't think I'm suffering any sort of concussion or anything: I really do think Dr Bushy looked relieved, and that Ms Dakota smiled at me in a proud way, like I'm the best pupil she'd ever had.

Well, she did say in art class today that I've made a lot of progress with my perspective.

'Uh, Olivia?' Sara said, sounding nervous. I think she was starting to realize she'd chosen the wrong lunch table. 'We'd better go. The bus is leaving.'

'Bus?' Sabine looked very insulted. 'Princess Olivia will *not* be riding the bus.'

Then she took me by the arm and began to steer me away from the group outside the school. To my surprise, I saw that not only were there three black town cars – each with tinted windows and miniature Genovian flags flying from them – waiting for me, but so were hordes of paparazzi. The paparazzi were behind a set of wooden barricades someone had erected to keep them off school property.

But that wasn't stopping them from using telephoto lenses.

Great. Every single one of them had probably got up-close photos of me getting my nose bashed in by Annabelle Jenkins.

'Are those cars for me?' I asked Sabine, hoping we could jump in one and get away as quickly as possible before anyone got any more embarrassing photos.

'And your security staff,' she said.

'Oh, good,' I said.

When we got to the middle town car, and Sabine opened the passenger door for me, I turned to look back at Cranford Middle School and noticed that everyone outside it was still watching me. It seemed like a good opportunity to use another one of the lessons Princess Mia had given me.

Even though my nose was killing me, I didn't want those reporters to think what Annabelle had done was bothering me. So, still pinching my nose and holding the tissues Ms Dakota had given me, I gave everyone at CMS a big Smile and Wave to let them know there were no hard feelings.

They all looked kind of confused for a minute, but then some of them waved back (and took photos with their phones, of course).

All except Nishi, who still looked super worried.

'Um,' I said to Sabine, through my frozen smile, 'do we have room for my friend Nishi to ride home with us?'

'Of course,' Sabine said, and spoke into her headset.

That's how Nishi ended up riding home with me in the town car. Riding in town cars isn't anywhere near as fun as riding in a limo (no mini-bar or disco lights), but it's still *way* more fun than riding on the bus.

Nishi got Sabine to show us all the cool stuff they have in Royal Genovian Guard town cars, like the police scanner and bulletproof windows (which don't roll down, so when Sabine let us stop at a drive-thru window – because I said my nose hurt so much that Nishi and I probably needed a chocolate milkshake to share – she had to get out of the car to get it).

Nishi made me hold a wad of cotton padding from the first aid kit pressed up to my nose – the whole ride home, even when we were sharing our milkshake. When we dropped her off at her house, she didn't want to leave.

'Are you *sure* you're going to be all right?' she asked before she got out of the car.

'Yes,' I said.

'Well, tell your aunt to make you an ice pack. Or maybe take you to the doctor,' Nishi said. 'Or do you want to come inside with me? My mom can take you.'

'It's OK,' I said. My voice still sounded strange, probably because I was still pinching my nose. 'We have ice. And I have these guys to take me to the doctor if I need to go.'

Sabine looked at Nishi from the front seat. 'I can assure you that we have the situation under control, Miss Patel.'

'OK,' Nishi said, still looking worried. 'But call me later, Olivia.'

'I will,' I assured her.

Nishi went into her house, and the Genovian Royal Guard drove me to mine, where I got out of the car to find Justin and Sara had just arrived as well. The bus had taken as long as a bulletproof four-door sedan that had made stops for milkshakes and to drop off my best friend.

'Ew,' Sara said, when she saw me. 'You're still all bloody.'

'Gross,' Justin said.

I don't know who was more surprised when we walked into the house to find my dad and Princess Mia sitting in the living room, talking to Aunt

Catherine and Uncle Rick – me or Justin and Sara.

'Oh, Olivia, there you are,' Aunt Catherine said as Snowball raced up to lick me hello. 'Your father wants to–'

It was right then that Mia stood up so fast, the cup of coffee she'd been balancing on a saucer on her knees fell to the floor and forever stained Aunt Catherine's pure white wall-to-wall carpeting.

'Oh my God!' Mia cried, rushing over and grabbing me. 'What happened to you? Where is that blood coming from?'

'Olivia.' Dad was right there beside her, running his fingers up and down my arms, as if he were looking for broken bones. 'Where are you hurt? Who did this to you?'

'She's OK,' Sara assured the adults as she picked up a gluten-free cookie from the plate on the coffee

table in front of her dad and stepmom. 'Annabelle Jenkins punched her in the face, is all.'

'My God,' Mia cried. She was trying to take the cotton padding away from my nose, but I wouldn't let her, because I didn't want to get blood on Aunt Catherine's white carpet. She was already on her hands and knees, trying to scrub out Princess Mia's coffee stain. 'Why didn't the Royal Genovian Guard stop her?'

'Dr Bushy said they had to stay fifty feet away from her,' I said, through the cotton padding. 'Annabelle's dad said he was going to sue the entire Cranbrook school district. Sabine said she called Lars to tell him to tell you, but he said that you were in a meeting. I didn't know the meeting was *here*.'

Both my dad and Mia turned to look accusingly at Lars, who was leaning against the living room wall. He reached up to tap his earpiece.

'You told me you didn't want to be disturbed, Your Highnesses,' he said with a sheepish shrug.

I could tell from my dad's expression that Lars was in really big trouble.

Still, I couldn't feel too worried for him. I couldn't feel too worried about *anything*. Instead, I was feeling hopeful. My dad was here! What did it mean? Something good. It had to. Right?

Except that Uncle Rick was laughing from his place on the couch. That didn't seem too good.

'Jenkins.' Uncle Rick shook his head. 'You gotta admit, the guy's good.'

Dad did not look as if he agreed with Uncle Rick.

'Oh dear,' Aunt Catherine said with a sigh from the carpet, where she was still scrubbing at the stain Princess Mia's spilled coffee had made. 'It's that preadolescent female aggression. They're at the age where it starts asserting itself.'

'In some girls, maybe,' Justin said with a smirk from where he was leaning in the kitchen doorway, also nibbling on a gluten-free cookie. 'Not in Olivia. You should have seen it. She went down like a tree.'

'You were there?' Dad whipped round to face Justin.

'Sure,' Justin said, looking surprised. 'Everybody was. Tons of photographers. They all got pictures.'

'Pictures?' Uncle Rick wasn't laughing any more.

'And you didn't do anything to stop it?' Dad barked at Justin.

'Well, I, um—' Justin looked scared. 'You know. It wasn't my fight.'

'So you just stood there and let Olivia get hit in the face?' Dad roared.

'Really, Phillipe.' Uncle Rick stood up and went to his son's side. 'It isn't my son's fault that your daughter can't take a—'

'He just said he was standing right there, watching the whole thing happen!' Dad shouted. 'What kind of boy would allow his own—'

'Please!' Aunt Catherine cried. 'What was Justin supposed to do? He has asthma!'

'I'm taking Olivia to a doctor right now,' Mia interrupted in a voice so cold I'm surprised it didn't freeze up the coffee stain Snowball was now sniffing.

'Oh, you don't have to do that,' Aunt Catherine said, looking embarrassed. Although I don't know by what. 'I'm sure our paediatrician—'

'You should notify your paediatrician that our

doctor in Genovia will be requesting Olivia's records,' Mia said, taking my hand. 'Because I believe this incident more than adequately proves the point we were discussing earlier: This isn't a safe – or stable – environment for Olivia to live in. If you disagree, you may contact *our* lawyers. Right, Dad? Come on, Olivia,' Mia said. 'Let's go get your things.'

She started tugging me towards my room, but even though my nose was throbbing, I wanted to see what was going to happen next.

Which is that my dad stopped glaring at Justin and Uncle Rick, and said, 'Yes. Yes, of course, Mia, you're right. Let's go.' He bent down to pick up Snowball.

'Isn't a stable environment for—' Aunt Catherine didn't look embarrassed now. She looked upset. 'After everything we've done for her!'

'I think you might want to have your lawyer review the documents in that file I've left on the coffee table, Catherine,' Dad said, holding a wriggling Snowball with one arm, 'before you continue bragging about what you've done for my daughter. Especially after what happened to her today.'

'But it – it was just a little fight,' Aunt Catherine stammered. 'A fight between girls! It was nothing!'

'Was it?' My dad's voice was cold. 'Because it doesn't look like nothing to me. In fact, considering what we now know about you and your husband's finances, as well as your dealings with this Jenkins person, it looks very much like *something* that I imagine you'd both like for us to drop instead of pursuing legally. Am I correct?'

I saw my aunt and uncle exchange a look. The look reminded me of the one Lars had worn earlier, of sheepish regret.

Still, Aunt Catherine wasn't willing to give up. She said, 'But I made a promise to my sister that I would raise her child to be as *normal* as possible—'

'Normal,' Dad asked icily, 'or *average*?'

When he asked this, Aunt Catherine's gaze fell to the floor . . . but not to Mia's coffee stain. To her feet. I saw her blush.

'You and I both know, Catherine,' Dad went on, 'that Elizabeth would never have wanted Olivia to be raised to be normal *or* average. She'd have wanted her to be raised to be *herself*, which is very far from average. And that's not what's happening around here, is it?'

Aunt Catherine looked up. Then, the next thing I knew, she was grasping my arms.

'Olivia,' she said, in a tearful voice, 'we never meant to make you feel average. I know we didn't spoil you, but that's because my sister wanted you to be raised like an ordinary girl, and to know what it's like to live amongst the common people. She didn't want you to grow up to be some snobby, rich princess who only cares about her looks and getting on the cover of magazines.' She narrowed her eyes at Princess Mia, who looked hurt. 'That's not what you want, is it, Olivia?'

'No,' I cried, horrified. 'Of course not!'

Aunt Catherine smiled. Her grip on my arms loosened a little. 'Oh, thank goodness,' she said. 'You had me worried!'

'I want to be a smart, brave, strong princess,' I declared, wrenching myself from her arms, 'who doesn't judge people by their looks, and who cares about people more than things! That's why I want to go live with them.' I pointed at my dad and sister.

Aunt Catherine stopped smiling when she heard this. She glanced at Uncle Rick, who looked as confused as she did.

'Olivia,' she said. 'What . . . what are you talking about? I care about you.'

'No, you don't. I know you don't. Because when I got home just now, Dad and Mia rushed over to see if I was all right. All *you* cared about was getting the stain out of your stupid carpet. So now that I've finally got some perspective, I'm going to go live with people who love me. Now, could someone please give me some ice? Because my nose really hurts.'

And now I'm holding the ice that Sabine got me over my nose as I write this, while she and Princess Mia pack up my stuff (not that there's so much of it), and Dad makes Aunt Catherine sign the papers giving up all legal guardianship of me.

Then we're going to get in the limo and drive away from Cranbrook forever.

But first Mia promised we could make one stop (after visiting a doctor for my nose. She insists), at a place I've always wanted to go:

The Cheesecake Factory.

Saturday 9 May
3.25 p.m.
Somewhere Over
the Atlantic Ocean

I am writing this on an aeroplane!

It's the first time I've ever been on an aeroplane in my whole entire life.

And it's not just *any* aeroplane – it's the Royal Genovian jet, a private plane just like the ones my mom used to fly.

Dad told me it was OK to go up into the cockpit and sit in the co-pilot's seat, and she let me wear her headset and talk to the control tower, and the pilot showed me all the controls and even let me steer for a while (until Grandmère sent a message up with one of the flight attendants that Rommel was feeling sick, and could I please stop).

This is definitely going on my list of best moments ever.

And guess what else? My nose doesn't even hurt any more. Well, except when I touch it. The nice doctor we went to see said it was only bruised, not broken.

And now the sovereign city-state of Genovia is suing Annabelle's dad! So that should be a nice change of pace for Mr Jenkins, his getting sued instead of doing the suing. His daughter punching me in the face at school has become the number one top trending story in the media. Between that, and Princess Mia's statement about how it was my dead mom who wanted my being a princess kept secret, the press has stopped asking me rude questions.

Grandmère says not to get used to it. She says, 'Everyone loves a scandal.'

I told her I'm going to try hard not to create any.

How can I, anyway? I'm on my way to my new home in Genovia, with my new family and my new dog, Snowball. Because this is a private plane, and the only people on it are my dad, Grandmère, Rommel, my sister and her husband-to-be, Michael (who is very nice and said he could tell I was going to make a very good aunt some day), I'm allowed to let Snowball sleep on my lap. She doesn't have to be in a dog carrier or anything.

I haven't seen Genovia yet outside my window, but I have seen the ocean and the tops of clouds.

I've never seen the tops of clouds before, only the sides and bottoms of them. The tops of them are so pretty, especially with the sun shining down on them, you can almost believe they're what heaven looks like, and that the angels are hiding behind all those piles of puffy whiteness, waiting until we've passed over (because we're not allowed to know angels exist until we're dead).

And then, as soon as we're out of sight, they're going to pop out again and go back to playing the harp or angel ping-pong or whatever it is angels do all day.

I'd wave to my mom in heaven out of the window,

but I don't want anyone to see me and ask who I'm waving to and then think I'm being weird, waving to the angel of my mom.

Besides, I don't have to wave. I think she already knows I'm here. And I'm pretty sure she's as happy for me as I am.

Sunday 10 May
5.00 p.m.
My Room,
Genovian Palace

I am very sleepy right now with something my dad says is called 'jet lag', which is what you get when you travel to a country which is in a time zone that isn't the same as the one you're used to (Genovia is six hours ahead of New Jersey, so I guess it's way past my bedtime right now).

But I just had to take a minute to write down that this is the *prettiest place I've ever seen*! Even though there is no Cheesecake Factory in Genovia, I obviously made the right decision coming here, and they have things that are just as good – if not better – than Cheesecake Factory, such as the royal kitchens, from which I can order *whatever I want, whenever I want it.*

I have already put in an order for waffles and eggs and soldiers for breakfast tomorrow morning. And also lunch.

Genovia even *smells* good, way better than Cranbrook. There are some kind of flowers blooming outside the balcony of my bedroom that smell like oranges.

That's because there *are* oranges growing there, on trees right outside my window! I can reach out whenever I want and pick one and eat it. FOR FREE. They do not charge for the oranges.

Or anything else. *Everything in the palace is free.* It is just like the limo, only much bigger, of course.

Did I mention my bedroom is huge and has hand-painted murals on the walls of clouds and birds (that are pretty realistic-looking, even if they're really old and weren't done by a wildlife illustrator), and also has its own balcony overlooking the palace pool?

Yes, we have our own
pool, which is filled with
fountains and looks out over
the ocean.

I knew Genovia was
going to be different than
Cranbrook, of course, but I
didn't know *how* different. I
already texted Nishi that she is
going to *freak out* when she gets
here because this place makes the
Beauty and the Beast castle at Disney
World look like the dump.

(Not that I've ever been to the Beauty
and the Beast castle, but I have been to the dump.
I went there a bunch of times with Aunt Catherine
and Uncle Rick to drop off waste from their
construction sites.)

Nishi hasn't texted back yet (probably because
of the time difference), but her parents already
said she could come for the ENTIRE summer
break, including for my sister's wedding, in which

we can *both* be junior bridesmaids.

I CANNOT WAIT (even if we do have to wear skirts, but Mia promised they would not be pleated).

Here's what else:

Genovia is right on the ocean, but not like the Jersey Shore is on the ocean. Genovia is built into these cliffs along the Mediterranean Sea, which is this beautiful turquoise blue, and the sand on the beaches is bright white, and there are these huge yachts and fancy restaurants and casinos and of course the PALACE, which has these big gold gates that we just drive right through because WE LIVE THERE.

And there are armed guards in funny blue-and-white costumes that stand guard outside the gates and that all the tourists takes photos of, but that Mia told me never to laugh at because they risk their lives to protect us, the royal family. I can respect that.

And Dad told me the palace doors

are made of wood that is nearly a thousand years old and there are portraits in the Great Hall of our ancestors dating back as far as the 1300s, and Grandmère said I am going to have to 'sit for a portrait' too, because now I am 'part of the family lineage'.

Which reminds me that I totally forgot to hand in my 'Who Am I?' worksheet in Bio.

But I guess it doesn't matter, since I've already been admitted to the Royal Genovian Academy. I'm going to start there soon, Dad says, but 'There's no rush. It's more important you get settled in to the new time zone – and your new family, of course – first.'

When he said that, I got a strange feeling. At first I didn't know what it was. Then I realized:

It was happiness. Family. I have a family, a real one, for the first time in my life.

This is the happiest moment of my life. Even happier than the day the art school called and said I'd been accepted with a full scholarship for my Tippy the Turtle drawing. Even happier than when

Dad asked me to come live with him.

And not because it turns out I'm a princess and I get to live in a beautiful palace on the ocean with orange trees right outside my window and birds painted on my walls.

It's not because I'm going to get to hang out with Nishi all summer, or even because I have a dog that's fast asleep on my lap, and she's MY dog to keep forever.

It's because I finally have a family that loves me.

And that's the least boring, least average, most special and most amazing thing of all.

The Royal Genovian Family Tree
By Olivia Grace

HRH Rosagunde
(1st Princess of Genovia)

HRH Clarisse Marie Grimaldi
Renaldo (Dowager Princess of
Genovia, aka Grandmère)

HRH Artur Gerard Christoff
Phillipe Grimaldi Renaldo
(71st Prince of Genovia,
aka Grandpère)

Lady Belle Beauty of Windenham
(Snowball's mom)

*Note: HRH stands for
Her (or His) Royal Highness*

HRH Genevieve
(17th Princess of Genovia)

HRH Mathilde the Brave
(21st Princess of Genovia)

HRH Artur Christoff Phillipe
Gerard Grimaldi Renaldo
(72nd Prince of Genovia, aka Dad)

Captain Elizabeth
Harrison (Mom)

HRH Amelia Mignonette Grimaldi
Thermopolis Renaldo (Mia)

HRH Olivia Grace Clarisse
Mignonette Harrison
Renaldo (Me!)

VISIT THE **GOBSTOPPERS** WEBSITE FOR

AUTHOR NEWS · BONUS CONTENT
VIDEOS · GAMES · PRIZES . . .
AND MORE!

MACMILLAN
Children's Books